"Wouldn't you like some of the lemonade? It's very good. Not too sweet."

He smiled, aware that she was ignoring him. "No, thank you. You were about to tell me about these other men you're dating."

Marcel laughed despite herself.

"I was about to do nothing of the sort." She started to rise.

He reached across the table, and before she could prevent it, captured one of her arms.

"Don't go," he said. His thumb gently stroked across her skin.

Marcel's eyes widened, but she remained where she was.

"Look at me."

Again, that strange authority in his voice. Marcel looked into his golden amber eyes. And what she saw caused a blend of fear and excitement to pound its way through her blood.

"What do you want from me?" she whispered.

His fingers slid down her arm to unclench her fingers. Then his thumb dipped to caress the soft center of her palm.

"I want . . . you," he said.

Praise for Niqui Stanhope and her novels

"Ms. Stanhope has built strong, graceful, and believable female characters."

—*Romantic Times*

"A taut, exciting romantic suspense that showcases Ms. Stanhope's unique literary talents . . . the story is a 'must-read.'"

—*Romantic Times* on *Distant Memories*

Changing the Rules

Niqui Stanhope

St. Martin's Paperbacks

CHANGING THE RULES

Copyright © 2003 by Monique Johnson.

All rights reserved. No part of this book may be used or reproduced in any manner whatsoever without written permission except in the case of brief quotations embodied in critical articles or reviews. For information address St. Martin's Press, 175 Fifth Avenue, New York, NY 10010.

ISBN: 0-312-98623-8

Printed in the United States of America

St. Martin's Paperbacks edition / October 2003

St. Martin's Paperbacks are published by St. Martin's Press, 175 Fifth Avenue, New York, NY 10010.

10 9 8 7 6 5 4 3 2 1

To all the women out there who fight the good fight! Don't give up. There is someone out there for you. Really. But you've got to believe!

Also for: Marcel Yansen, a childhood friend I haven't forgotten.

Prologue

Marcel Templeton pushed a swatch of hair out of her eyes and reached for the phone.

"Oh, Alex," she said sweetly, when she heard her boyfriend of almost eleven months on the other end. "I didn't think you'd call me this early."

A little smile touched the corners of her lips for a second. Over the past several months, she and Alex Baker had definitely seen their fair share of problems. In the last week in particular, things had been very rocky. He had been moody and disagreeable, and she had caught him on more than one occasion openly eyeing other women. Sometimes she actually felt as though she was the only one who wanted the relationship to work. But he could be sweet and considerate, too, when the mood took him. And calling her at the crack of dawn on her birthday just so she might start the day on a happy note was definitely one of those very thoughtful things that he did from time to time. He knew how important this birthday was to her and how much she had been secretly dreading it. Turning thirty was a significant event in any woman's life. And it was particularly significant if the woman was still unmarried and childless.

"I'm sorry . . . what was that you said, honey?" Marcel asked, and she gave the alarm clock sitting on her bedside table a quick look. Seven o'clock. It was earlier than she had thought.

"I was saying . . . I hope you have a happy birthday today, baby. You know I want only the very best for you."

Marcel smiled. "Thank you, sweetie. That's so nice of you." She paused for a moment and then went on in a thoughtful voice. "Thirty years old, though. I can't even believe it myself. It seems like just the other day I was graduating from college. A kid. It's just incredible how quickly the time can go—"

"Yes," Alex interrupted. "And that's part of the reason why I'm calling, too. There's something important we need to talk about."

Marcel's heart gave a sudden thud in her chest and her palms went damp and cold. He wanted to talk to her about something important? At the crack of dawn on her birthday? It could only be one thing. But why would he choose to propose on the phone?

It wasn't at all romantic. This wasn't the way she had envisioned it. But a proposal was a proposal, so she wouldn't give him a hard time about it.

She cuddled the phone close. He couldn't have given her a better birthday gift. What a way to start this most important year of her life—with a wedding to look forward to.

"Go ahead, sweetheart. I'm listening." She closed her eyes and crossed her fingers. Alex was far from perfect, but she was old enough now to understand that everyone had their flaws. And maybe Alex's little problems had more to do with the fact that he was still quite immature. But all of that would change with time. And she would help him change. She would work very hard at building a life with him. She didn't really love him in the traditional sense of the word, of course. But that was all right. Real love would come in time. . . .

"I . . . I. . . ."

"Yes, honey?" Marcel urged, impatient now that he should get it over with. There would be so many arrangements to make. She was going to splurge on the wedding dress. She could see it already. Wonderful white satin, edged with lace and pearls. A high neckline. A long, wispy train. It was going to be beautiful and her mother, her mother was going to be so happy. Her girlfriend Tracy would go into total and complete shock, of course, because it had always been her opinion that Alex was not a marrying kind of guy.

"I think we should see other people."

The gush of words was so sudden and so unexpected that for a moment Marcel just stared blankly at the phone in her hand.

"What?" she managed after a few unsuccessful attempts at speech. There was a faint buzzing in her ears and she felt as though every trace of blood had just left her head.

His voice was suddenly stronger. "Things just aren't working out, Marcel." His voice became coaxing. "You know it. I know it. And if you're truthful you know you've been thinking the same thing." He sighed and Marcel closed her eyes. This couldn't be happening to her. Not today of all days.

"What you really need is a different kind of guy . . . someone who'll love you the right way. The way you deserve to be loved. He'll . . . he'll do all those little things you like. Besides, you're getting older and—"

Her eyes snapped back open and the beginnings of rage sparkled somewhere in their depths. "And you don't want me anymore because of it. Right? You want someone younger and you decided to save this little surprise for my birthday."

She listened in cold silence as his voice became an apologetic whine.

"Don't bother to explain," she cut him off. "I really don't want to hear it." And without another word, she slammed the phone back into its cradle and then flopped back against the pillows. She was too angry to cry. Too angry to even feel. Of all the things Alex had ever done, this was definitely the worst. What kind of man telephoned on your thirtieth birthday, wished you happy birthday, and then, just as calmly as you please, informed you that he no longer wanted to see you? And to think she had actually believed that he had been about to propose marriage. How ridiculous! How pathetic.

She pounded her pillow with a fist. God, why did this keep happening to her? What did she keep doing wrong? What? It was the same thing relationship after relationship. Why did men never stay with her? Why did they always leave? And when would she ever find a nice, normal guy who wanted at least some of the same things she did?

The ringing of the phone brought her out of volcanic thought and she cast a malevolent glare in its direction. It was Alex calling again, of course. She was very familiar with this pattern. It was always the same. He would do something completely outrageous, they would have a huge fight, and then he would come crawling back to her, begging her forgiveness and promising never to hurt her again. Well, not this time. Not for any reason under the sun would she ever take him back again. Not after this.

She snatched the phone up and asked in a hard little voice, "Yes? Who is this?"

The voice in her ear was warm and bright, and Marcel took a deep breath. Her *mother*. She was so not in the right mood to deal with her at the moment. Not with her entire life in complete shambles around her.

"Hi, Mom," she said, and a twinge of guilt crept into her voice. It wasn't her mother's fault that Alex had just broken up with her, after all.

Her brow wrinkled as she listened with half an ear to her mother's voice. She sucked in a breath after a moment and said in a very flat voice, "No, Mom, I don't have anything romantic planned. Nothing at all."

She didn't want to go into it right then. She didn't feel at all up to rehashing the details of the breakup. It was too fresh and her mother would somehow find a way to make her feel that everything had been all her fault.

"I'm just going to spend the day quietly. No, not with Alex." That was as far as she would go right then. Tomorrow, she would call her and explain that Alex was gone for good.

"I really don't think he cares one way or the other, Mom. Besides—" Her mother cut her off and Marcel let her speak until it became impossible to hold the words at bay any longer. "I'm not being mean-spirited. And yes, of course I want to get married, but it's hard. Things are rough out there. It's not like when you were young. Most of the available men have problems. And I'm not talking about anything you can fix in a few sessions of psychotherapy, either. I mean they have serious, serious problems."

Her mother interrupted once more, but Marcel charged on this time, determined not to be swayed from her course.

"Like what problems? Well, let me tell you. They're all chronic liars for one. Especially the good-looking ones like Alex. Those are the worst, the absolute worst, of the entire bunch. They try to put on this ridiculous 'nice guy' routine. But the reality of it is . . . they're . . . they're nothing but the devil in disguise."

Marcel clicked her tongue in irritation when it became clear that her mother was refusing to go along with her take on things. "Yes, they are, Mom. They're evil, I tell you. I've dated more than enough of them to know at least that. And no, it's not just California men, either. I've dated men from New York, Atlanta, D.C. . . . . you name it. They're all exactly the same. It doesn't matter where they come from. As long as they're a man—"

She sank onto the side of the bed and listened with forced patience as her mother went off on a long ramble about how many really good men there were left and how even if Marcel and Alex didn't end up making a life together, she was bound to find a good man if only she would just believe that he was out there for her.

"Well, I don't know about that, Mom," Marcel finally said, shaking her head and sending her hair into a wild mess about her shoulders. "I don't think there's a single solitary *good* man left out there. Nice guys only exist in the movies. And that's the plain truth. Take it from me. I've had some *nice guys* in my time and I know what they're really like." She brushed a swatch of hair behind an ear. "From now on I'm steering clear of all men who seem a little too good to be true. It would be so much easier if I could just once and for all . . . give them up completely."

She cleared her throat and frowned heavily as her mother cackled with laughter.

"I'm very serious about it, Mom," she said. "Life would be so much easier if I could only learn how to live completely without a man in my life. I mean, I'm an independent woman. I pay my own bills. Have my own house. My own car. Why do I have to . . . to keep going through all of this aggravation? I have never had a relationship where I didn't have to go through some sort of drama. And if you want to know the truth, I'm getting really tired of—"

Her mother cut her off neatly, and Marcel propped the phone between the side of her jaw and her shoulder and resigned herself to listening to her mother's philosophy on life. There was no point in explaining things any further, she realized. Her mother would never understand. She was from a different era. A different time. A time when men were, perhaps, totally different creatures.

Marcel held on to a deep sigh as the usual pep talk was trotted out for her benefit: She was an attractive young woman. A very attractive young woman. One whom any man would be proud to have as his wife. But it was just that she was too much of a career woman. And running her father's old magazine with a skeleton staff didn't help things, either. And maybe, just maybe, she wasn't trying hard enough. Didn't she want to have children? Maybe Alex wasn't the right man for her. But there were lots of other men. Lots of other men. But the only way she was going to find one was if she was open to finding him. And she couldn't possibly hope to do this if she spent most of her waking hours locked away behind closed doors. The only way she was ever going to meet a new man at all was if he happened to skydive through her bedroom or office window. . . .

After half an hour of this, Marcel hung up with cold and trembling hands. She got off the bed and shuffled across to the bathroom in her shabby terry cloth slippers. It wasn't her mother's fault, of course. She was only trying to help. How was she to know the rush of cold unadulterated terror that her little pick-me-up talks inevitably brought?

Marcel was probably going to end up a lonely snaggletoothed old hag with a hump on her back. And who would want her then? Nobody. That's who.

Marcel nodded and muttered peevishly. Sure, her mother could say that there were lots of good men left out there. But where were they all hiding? Was there a club somewhere out there where they all hung out, laughing among themselves at the travails of poor females like her?

She stomped into the bathroom, closed the door behind her, and barely managed to stifle a terrified shriek. Oh God, it was beginning to happen already. Who was that wild-haired, red-eyed hag staring back at her? Surely that was not her? She looked at her reflection once, then again. Was that a wrinkle beneath her eye? Surely not yet? Surely not so very soon? Her heart pounded with dread, and she grabbed wildly for a bottle of Olay anti-aging cream, scooped a good portion into her hand, and then massaged the offending area with great vigor.

With lotion slathered all over her face and neck, she got onto the scale, a daily ritual she never failed to observe. A smudge of lotion tickled the corner of an eye, and she rubbed it away with the back of a hand and blinked at the scale. *Five pounds?* How had she managed to gain five whole pounds in just under eight hours? Wasn't that impossible?

A fine sheen of perspiration broke out across her brow. She had heard about the age-related slowing of the metabolic rate, but this was simply incredible. What would be the next thing to go? Her hair? Her teeth?

Marcel spent careful minutes wiping her skin free of the thick layer of lotion, then stepped into the shower and turned the water on full blast. Her brain churned as she lathered and loofahed. There were no two ways about it. She had to find herself a new man. She had to. Time, quite frankly, was running out.

She sat on the side of the tub and scrubbed at her heels with a piece of white pumice stone. Why in the name of God had she not noticed the days going by? Why had she not realized how quickly it would all change? Just the other day she'd been twenty-five. Young. Carefree. *Beautiful even.*

She scrubbed viciously at a stubborn patch of skin. But what was she now? A balding old spinster with loose teeth and a butt the size of Texas.

A frown marred the smooth skin between her eyes. It was almost enough to make her give the whole thing up. Why wait? She could buy herself a rocking chair and some knitting or, better yet, just check herself into a retirement home and wait for her entire body to fall apart.

She stood with a flourish, her hair wet, frizzy, her eyes brightly determined. What was she talking about? What was she saying? She had never given up on anything before in her life. And she wasn't about to give up on herself now. She was a winner. And no matter how Alex had tried to hurt her, she would get around this. There *was* a special man waiting somewhere out there just hoping and praying for someone like her. And she was determined to find him even if she had to extend a leg and trip him herself once she ran into him. . . .

Chapter One

Marcel gave her watch a quick look and then leaned heavily on the horn.

"Come on! Come on!" she bellowed at the vehicle just in front of her. She had been stuck behind the same white monstrosity for the past several miles and had been forced to creep along the main street out of downtown San Diego at about twenty miles per hour. At this rate she would never make it to Versailles and back to her office in time to finish the mountain of work she still had to complete before the launch of the next issue of *La Beau Monde*. Why had she let Tracy talk her into lunch now? She had no time for this sort of thing. Not now.

She leaned on the horn again. What was wrong with the idiot driver anyway? Didn't he understand that when the lights turned amber everyone sped up?

No one at all in his or her right mind actually slowed down at an intersection when the lights were about to change.

Her gaze flickered over the license plate and her mouth tightened in disgust. An out-of-towner. Of course. The man was probably out having a great time sightseeing or maybe he was just plain lost. Well, either way, she had absolutely no more time to spend inching along behind him. She was going to have to take drastic measures. And she would do so at the next light.

The white truck dropped another five miles per hour, and Marcel muttered a heated, "That's it!"

She pulled her little Toyota onto the right shoulder of the road and then stepped hard on the gas. The car responded to her touch like a racehorse that had been reined in for far too long. In a burst of speed, she pulled alongside the offensive white vehicle and prepared to dart into the lane ahead. But, just as suddenly, the white truck canted to the right and began to turn.

Marcel leaned hard on the horn and bellowed out the window of the car, "No, no! You can't turn, you idiot! Are you blind? I'm over here. I'm over here!"

But the driver paid her scant attention and continued his turn as though he hadn't a care in the world.

Marcel stepped hard on the brake as the white side of the pickup truck loomed almost directly before her. She could just see it now, her broken and twisted body sprawled all over the curb and the lunatic in the truck, the one who had caused the whole mess, would probably escape the entire ordeal without a single scratch in place.

She hung on to the steering wheel with eyes closed as the wheels locked. *Please, God. Please, God. Please, God.* If she ended up with an entire mouthful of dentures or a severed leg or something, not even the most kindhearted man in the world would want her then. She would have to resort to eating soft food and hobbling and thumping her way around with her one-and-a-half leg. Then, before she knew it, she would probably start losing huge chunks of hair, and of course she would start going blind, too.

A loud bang on the driver's side window caused her eyes to spring open. Thank God. The car had stopped moving, and she wasn't maimed or dead or something.

"Good God. Are you OK? Don't you know that you're not supposed to drive on the shoulder of the road? Are you trying to kill yourself?"

Marcel placed a nicely manicured finger on the control panel and eased the window by just a crack. *Was she trying to kill herself?* Was he actually accusing her of almost causing her own dismemberment or death?

"Don't you know how to drive?" she countered in a very steady voice, and her gaze rose to meet two of the most gorgeous male eyes she had ever seen. "There is a minimum speed requirement on most of these roads, you know."

The man pressed a hand to the side of his head and muttered something about women drivers that caused Marcel's blood pressure to rise by several notches. *So, he is a chauvinist too.*

"Are you hurt?"

Marcel's chin tilted. "No, I am not hurt. But no thanks to you, of course. Didn't you see me beside you when you started to turn? Don't you use your side-view mirrors?"

Her gaze flickered over him as she spoke and his masculine beauty brought a flush of hot blood to her face. Lord, but he was a fine-looking man. He was tall. Definitely over six feet. Had smooth brown skin. Unusually beautiful amber eyes. A broad chest. Hard, flat stomach. White T-shirt. Faded blue jeans. Curly black hair. Wonderful lips. . . .

"Well, I'm glad you're OK. I never would've forgiven myself if I'd injured you in any way." His voice snapped her out of her sudden fantasy of sweet, hot kisses.

She blinked at him and swallowed away the ridiculous dryness in the back of her throat. "What?"

"You're not hurt," he said again in a very patient voice. "And you haven't done much damage to my truck, so I don't think we need to make this formal. Of course, if you want to make it up to me, maybe you'd like to have dinner one evening this week? My name is Ian Michaels, by the way." And he gave her a sexy, confident smile that made Marcel grit her teeth. *A player*. Of course. She'd had her fill of those.

She drew in a tight breath and leaned forward to turn the key in the ignition. God, how she despised men who played fast and loose with a woman's affection. Never, never again would she ever have anything to do with any of them. They were all invariably immoral, lying, dirty dogs. And this tall, brown Adonis standing at her car window was no different. He probably had a wife hidden somewhere or, more likely, an entire legion of baby mamas scattered around the city and state.

She didn't offer her name but instead said in a very precise manner, "Thank you for being so . . . understanding. But since this incident was entirely your fault, you'll have to excuse me if I'm not overly grateful."

Marcel turned the key and the engine purred softly to life. The man stepped back from the car window and stood there looking down at her with an expression of hard speculation in his amber eyes.

Marcel gave him another flickering glance through the half-open window, and even though she was still smarting from her recent dumping, she had to admit that this man was one tall package of temptation. He was long and hard, with beautifully muscled legs, and appeared to possess exactly the kind of physical characteristics that on a normal day would have made her think twice before turning down an invitation to dinner . . . and maybe even more than twice, if she was completely honest about it.

She shook herself. What was she thinking? If this guy wasn't Alex all over again, then her mama wasn't a matchmaker. No, she wanted nothing more to do with any men like him.

"So, you're turning down my invitation to dinner?"

Marcel gave him a direct look. He sounded surprised. He had probably never been rejected before. Well, the experience could do him some good. It might even help him understand that he couldn't have every single woman he laid eyes on.

"I'm turning it down." She favored him with a little smile. "If I were you, though, I'd spend some time working on my driving skills and not so much time trying to pick up the women you run down."

A smile flickered in his amber eyes and a surprising dimple appeared in his left cheek and then just as quickly disappeared.

"As far as my driving skills go, you almost ran into me, young lady," he said, a note of lazy amusement in his voice. "And, believe me, I don't usually *pick up* women I run into on the street. Not that I run into all that many."

Marcel nodded. Right. A likely story. But how could he know that she'd met his type many, many times before?

"Good luck to you," she said, not bothering to argue the point with him. "And just remember that a minimum speed of thirty miles per hour is recommended on these busy downtown streets." And with that said, she roared back into the noonday traffic.

As she very nearly ran down another car, she noticed that there was a child in the front seat of his pickup. The expression on her face hardened. How right she had been to turn down his invitation to dinner. It was baby mama drama all over again. . . .

Chapter Two

Versailles was a jewel of a restaurant sitting atop a grassy swell on Harbor Island. It was perched on a ridge of land just overlooking the glittering blue of San Diego Bay, and on most days it was next to impossible to secure a lunch reservation there.

Ian Michaels turned his white truck into the curving drive of willowy palms, cut the sputtering motor with a gentle twist of his hand, climbed out, walked around to the passenger side, then lifted the little girl down from the passenger seat.

The child looked up at him with vaguely impatient eyes. "But you promised me a hamburger and ice cream, Uncle Ian."

"You'll get your hamburger," Ian promised, and he gave the tip of her nose a fond little tap. "But

Uncle wants to talk to that nice lady we just saw a little while ago. OK?"

The child gave him a doubtful look. "Do we have to stay long?"

"Come on, you little worrywart. I promise you it'll be fun. Trust me?"

A parking attendant materialized from the confines of a fashionably thatched hut at almost that exact moment and the child's attention was distracted by his very cheerful, "Well, hello there. Aren't you a pretty little thing? What's your name?"

"Go on. Tell him your name," Ian urged. "She's a bit shy," he said to the man.

"I am not shy," she objected. "My name is Daniella Michaels. But everyone calls me Dani for short."

The parking attendant shook the outstretched hand in a grave manner while Ian did his best not to let the smile he was feeling show on his face. His niece was a force unto herself. There was no question about that.

"Put the truck in a good spot, would you?" Ian said.

"It was my daddy's truck," Daniella added helpfully.

The valet grinned and nodded. "Don't worry. I'll find a very special spot for it, OK?"

Ian pressed a folded twenty-dollar bill into the man's hand and allowed his gaze to drift in a leisurely manner about the parking lot. When he found what it was he sought, his lips curled at the corners. He had followed her at a distance and had been pleased to discover that she was having lunch at one of his favorite restaurants. Now he intended to see for himself who it was she was lunching with. He was a firm believer in thoroughly researching the competition before launching any form of attack. And attack he would, using every weapon in his collective arsenal.

A slight furrow appeared between his brows. She would be lunching with a man, of course. Possibly a boyfriend or someone she was currently dating casually. He had noticed that she did not wear a ring. So it was more than likely that she wasn't involved in a serious relationship. Whoever it was, though, would be dispatched with all possible speed. It had been many years since any woman had managed to capture his interest in this way. But the mystery woman had actually made him laugh, and it had been a long time since he had done even that. And when she had turned down his invitation to dinner, her fate had been sealed. She had aroused his hunter's instinct without even realizing what it was she had done. In that very moment, he had decided that he would have her. And he would do so before the close of this very month. That was a promise.

"Come on, Dani," he said. And he took the child's hand and walked briskly up the short flight of whitewashed stairs. He was greeted at the entrance by the maître d'.

Much was made over the little girl again, and then the headwaiter asked pleasantly, "Would you like your usual table overlooking the bay, Mr. Michaels?"

Ian's amber eyes swept the sea of nicely arranged foam green tables. "No, I'd like that table over there, Pierre. Behind the large potted fern."

The maître d' nodded. "Ah . . . I see. Yes, of course. Come with me, please."

After they were comfortably seated and the headwaiter had left to attend to another table, Ian pressed his finger to his lips to still the child's curious question and gently parted one of the large fronds before him. His lips curled in pleasure at what he saw on the other side of the plant. The mystery woman was seated just a few paces before him. And she was not lunching with a man. . . .

On the other side of the giant pot, Marcel gave the trembling leaf of the large fern a distracted glance.

"I know what you're saying," she said after a minute more spent staring at the plant. "But I don't know if I'm ready to start dating again just yet."

Tracy gestured with a bread stick. "Girl, you can't bury yourself in that magazine of yours. You've gotta find some time to get out and start looking again. How else are you going to run into Mr. Wonderful?"

Marcel snorted. "Mr. Wonderful. Right. You know I always end up choosing the wrong man."

Tracy gave her a sympathetic look. "Everyone has an Alex in their life at one point in time or another. But that doesn't mean you stop trusting your instincts, you know what I mean? You're a great judge of character."

Marcel drew breath to object and Tracy waved away her protests with, "You are. You just chose the wrong man this time out. But that's OK. Everyone's entitled."

Marcel gave an unconvinced, "Hmm," then paused to stir her glass of iced tea with a sugared swizzle stick. "What I really want to know is, How come nothing's ever easy for me? I mean, why do I have to suffer like this all the time? You know? Why does nothing ever just fall right into my lap?" She gestured with a hand. "Take this whole finding a man thing. I see tons of women every day with good relationships. With good men. And I look at them and think, 'Now why can't that be me?'"

Tracy adjusted the stylish glasses on her face, and for just a moment, her eyes became intent. "Maybe you're looking for a perfect man, Marcy, honey. And the simple truth is, he just doesn't exist."

Marcel pursed her lips. "Well, I know that's right.

I've had more than enough of men who seem all nice and normal in the beginning, but a few months down the road you've got nothing but the very devil in disguise."

Tracy broke a bread roll and spread one half with garlic butter. "What you need is the kind of man who'll make you feel all warm inside. The kind who will rub your back when it's sore . . . make you chicken soup when you're sick. Cook for you every now and again. . . ."

Marcel crunched on a bread stick. "God, yes. That's exactly what I need. And girl, you know I was never one to pay too much attention to this whole biological clock thing. But of late . . . I don't know if it's turning thirty that's getting to me or the fact that this whole not being able to find a man thing's making my mother completely crazy." She took another sip of iced tea. "Truthfully, I've got more important things to worry about. Business things. I don't need this kind of aggravation."

Tracy nodded and gave a noncommittal "Hmm."

Marcel sighed. "You know I love my mother to death. But sometimes she just drives me crazy. She means well, but . . . every single time she calls? The same exact thing? And she doesn't understand how hard it is out there. It's not like there's a pile of eligible bachelors just standing around waiting to be scooped up. It's hard to find a good man these days. I mean, it's *really* hard." She nodded at the waiter as he placed a plate of steaming chicken fettuccine before her. "But I don't expect you to understand what I mean. You've been married for too long, and not only that, you've got yourself one of the few really good men in existence."

Tracy moved her glass out of the way and rested both elbows on the table. "You didn't know Tommy in the early days," Tracy said. "You think he *wanted* to get married?" Two elegant eyebrows climbed toward her hairline. "Please. No man *wants* to get married. Messing around is in their blood. But," and she leaned forward to whisper in a conspiratorial manner, "the *good* ones can be trained."

"I don't know. . . ."

Tracy waved an authoritative finger in the air. "Trust me on this one, OK? Men *have* to be trained. *All men*. Even the good ones. They really don't know how to do the right thing on their own. It's just not in their nature to behave that way. And don't think for a minute that the problems are over once you get them down the aisle."

Marcel took a bite of creamy chicken. "I just don't know what to do. I'm so confused. I don't seem to have what it takes to really hold a man . . . for any length of time. I don't know what it is. Everything usually starts out fine, and then . . . just as it did with Alex . . . they begin to lie and sneak around. . . ."

"Girl, Alex was just a dog, OK? Accept it and

move on. I told you from the very first time I met him what he was like. But you were all in lust and everything. And would you listen to me?"

"Well . . ."

"Don't give me that 'well' business. You know I'm right. You have to be willing to see the signs right from the start. The fact that it didn't work out between you two didn't have a thing to do with you. He had some issues to work out. You know what I mean? Count yourself lucky that things didn't get really serious."

Marcel took a measured sip of water, gave the large fern before her another look, and then continued.

"I just know I'm going to end up old and alone in an old folks' home somewhere."

A loud spate of coughing coming from somewhere behind the fern made Tracy turn and cast a glance over her shoulder.

She turned back after a moment and said in a lowered voice, "Look, Marcy honey, we may all end up old, alone, and in an old folks' home. But that has nothing to do with getting and keeping a man."

Marcel waited for a passing waiter to go by and then leaned forward to hiss, "I know that. But knowing something and making it happen are two totally different things. I want to get married. Who wants to end up old and alone with nobody around to care for you? But the thing is, if I wait too much longer,

I just know that my whole body's going to start falling apart. You know what I mean? And how can I have kids if I'm half-blind and I've got arthritis in my hip or something? In that sort of condition, I don't even think I'd be able to make it through labor." She leaned forward to take another sip from her glass. "You think I'm kidding? It's not like I'm just bursting with youth anymore. This is serious. Right now as we speak, it even feels like my teeth are beginning to loosen at the roots."

Tracy's eyes sparkled with amusement. "You'd better stop talking crazy. If you have arthritis at your age, you'd better check yourself into a hospital, and fast. Anyway," she continued without giving Marcel a chance to say a word, "we *are* going to find a man for you. But when we find him, if he's husband material," and she paused to wag a finger, "you have to promise that you won't start looking for every reason in the book why you can't marry him, all right?"

Marcel pursed her lips. "Every reason in the book? Is it my fault that most men have serious personality problems?"

Tracy gave her an "Um-hmm, girl. Men will be men," and then leaned forward to say with great enthusiasm, "But you have to work with whatever you've got." She adjusted her glasses with the tip of her index finger. "First thing you have to do if you really want to get a man is calm down. Men will run at the first scent of panic and desperation. So, you have to be cool about it. You have to make them think that you don't really care about this marriage thing, one way or the other. You see, men divide women into two groups: easy game and hard game . . . because essentially they know what we all want." She smiled at Marcel's skeptical look. "That's right, they do. And because they do, they play with us. They'll promise the women they see as 'easy game' everything under the sun until they get what they want. But they won't stick around for long after they get it. You know what I mean?"

Another session of coughing from behind the fern caused Marcel to roll her eyes and say, "I hope to God that whatever he's got isn't contagious. My body can't deal with anything else right now. It's already trying to fight off old age."

"Try to focus for just half a minute," Tracy said, waving a dismissive hand. "What I'm trying to tell you here is more important than a few germs. OK? So listen to me. Getting a man to marry you is easy—if you understand how they think. Men are simple animals, you see. They'll chase, they'll love, they'll settle down with the woman they see as 'hard game.' " She tapped the smooth tabletop with a finger to emphasize her point. "If you want to get a man, and keep him, you have to know this little truth: You can't make this thing too easy for them. They're hunters. You know? So, you have to make them work for it. Make them hunt. If you do that, they'll put a ring on your finger so fast, even you won't be able to believe it."

Marcel frowned. "But I hate playing games."

Tracy took a hefty bite from her bread roll and wiped away a smear of butter from the corner of her mouth with a colorful paper napkin. "That's why you don't have a man. This is the real world, honey. If you want a husband, really want a husband, then you've got to play the game."

Marcel was silent for a moment. Maybe Tracy was right. What did it matter if it all sounded completely superficial? If she ended up with a man at the end of the entire thing, who would know or even care how it was she had actually gotten him?

She looked up from her plate of rapidly cooling noodles to find her friend watching her. "Well, what d'you think I should do?"

Tracy smiled in a very pleased manner. "I'm glad you asked. What you need is a kind of dating security blanket. A list of rules to help you make the right choices."

Marcel fiddled with her noodles. "You know, maybe you're right. It would be so much easier if I knew exactly what to look for, wouldn't it?"

Tracy nodded. "Until you start feeling really comfortable about the choices you make, I think it'd be really helpful."

"Hmm," Marcel agreed. "You know, all through

my twenties I kept hoping and praying that the right man would just come along. Just appear one day. I even imagined different ways I might meet him. You know? Like maybe in the grocery store late one night, while I was shopping for an item I had forgotten earlier in the day. . . ."

Tracy shook her head. "You're too much of a romantic."

Marcel nodded. "I know. It'd be so nice, though, if I could find my one true love by the time I turn thirty-three. So that by about . . . thirty-five, I have at least one kid. Boy, girl, it doesn't really matter."

Tracy beamed. "And with 'the rules,' you *will* find him, girl. I promise you."

A waiter appeared at that very moment to ask if they were enjoying the meal, and Tracy shooed the man away with a flick of her hand and then commented in an undertone, "Don't you hate it when they do that? I mean, does he actually think he'll get a bigger tip if he comes by the table every two minutes?"

Marcel chuckled. "Leave the poor guy alone. He was just trying to be nice and attentive. I'm sure he wasn't just thinking about his tip."

Tracy shrugged. "Whatever." And she rifled around in her handbag and then pulled out a pen and a piece of paper. "Now about these rules."

Chapter Three

Ian Michaels, comfortably seated on the other side of the fern, settled in to listen, too. He wasn't at all disturbed by the fact that for the past half an hour he'd been eavesdropping on the conversation between the two women. In fact, he'd been so amused at various parts of the little tête-à-tête that he'd been forced to quell the laughter bubbling in his chest with several very loud coughs. Waves of humor had rocked him so hard and fast that the maître d' had become extremely alarmed and had rushed over to pound Ian on the back. It had taken quite a bit of doing to convince the man that he was in fact in perfect health and did not require the Heimlich maneuver performed on him.

He sat back in his chair now with furrowed brows and fingers steepled beneath his chin. Marcel. An interesting name for an interesting woman. She was going to be a far more complex conquest than he had originally thought. He was surprised that a woman of such obvious attractiveness should have any difficulty finding a suitable partner. She was an unmistakable beauty. Above average in height, thick in the thigh, and heavy in the bosom. Any man of normal appetite would be driven to drink at the mere thought of not having her. Her lips were plump and softly inviting. And her long creamy brown legs were enticing enough to draw the gaze of a blind man. They had drawn his eyes and had sparked an excitement in him that had taken him by complete surprise.

Her most powerful feature, though, was, without question, her eyes. They were almond-shaped, tar black, and tilted at the corners in an almost feline manner. He was no stranger to beautiful women, but it had taken no more than a glance from her to fire his blood and his loins. Wild and unbidden thoughts had flashed through him as his eyes had met hers. He had imagined running the flat of his palm in slow circles up the soft swell of her inner thigh. He had seen her lying in the center of his king-size bed, soft skin glowing like honey in the firelight, lips parted in soundless pleasure, as he showed her how sweet, how fierce, how absolutely satisfying lovemaking could be. It had all been so crystal clear to him that he'd been convinced that the reason she'd turned his dinner invitation down was that she had somehow known his thoughts, too, and had feared the uncontrollable passion that would surely burn between them.

Daniella, with a smear of ice cream about her mouth, interrupted his train of thought for a minute with a half-impatient, "Uncle, are we going soon?"

"Soon," Ian promised, and leaned slightly forward as the women's voices lowered. It would obviously be no easy task getting close to Marcel Templeton, but he would do it. He was very interested in listening to these rules, though. They might prove to be the key to unraveling her resistance to him. A tight little smile touched the corners of his lips. In fact, he welcomed her struggle. He was the kind of man who enjoyed a good challenge, because, in the end, she would be his. He would win. He always did.

Marcel gave the surrounding tables a quick glance. "Do you think we should go into the rules here, though? It's such a public place, and someone might—"

"Please," Tracy said, interrupting her with a wave of her hand. "No one's listening to us. Besides, even if someone did overhear a few words here and there, would they know what we're talking about?"

"Hmm," Marcel agreed. "But—"

Tracy waved the pen. "No buts. You're not going

to put this off. I know exactly what you're trying to do."

Marcel dabbed at a bead of perspiration on the tip of her nose and gave her friend a heated look. "God, you're such a pain."

"I know and I don't care. Rule number one."

Marcel chuckled despite herself. "OK. OK. Rule number one. What've you got?"

"First," Tracy said, and she tapped the pen in a thoughtful manner against the round of her chin. "Let's start with the really practical things. Equipment. And don't even try to tell me that you don't care about it. Every woman cares, OK? *Every woman.* And the ones who say they don't, they're all lying."

Marcel's mouth popped open and she struggled with laughter. "You're not serious. You're going to make *that* a rule?"

Tracy lifted two perfectly groomed eyebrows. "Believe me, you need a man who's got the tools and knows how to use them, too. He's got to know how to handle himself. You know what I mean?" And she looked at Marcel for confirmation. "It's important. And you have to be certain of these things before you even think of marrying a man. After all, you're not going to have access to anyone else for the rest of your life, am I right? So," she said, not waiting for a response, "you'd better make sure that you get exactly what you want, then. This is a life-time thing we're talking about."

Marcel chuckled merrily. "So, what're we talking about? Six inches?"

Tracy gave it a moment of thought. "Six to eight in length. And about two inches in girth. More than two inches is OK, of course. But for good performance, you have to have at least two."

The sound of Marcel's laughter echoed above the soft noise of conversation and cutlery, and Tracy shushed her with, "What? You think girth isn't important? You want him to be good between the sheets, don't you?"

Marcel nodded. "Well, of course. That's a given."

Tracy beamed. "OK then. So, if we're going to be really scientific about this thing, then we have to consider everything. You know what I mean?"

"And how am I supposed to properly judge length and girth?" Marcel asked, her eyes sparkling with amusement.

"Two things," Tracy said, leaning forward to whisper. "And this is a secret my grandmother passed on to me a while ago, but believe me, in the years since, it's rarely failed me."

"Um-hmm," Marcel said, great interest in her voice. "What'd she say?"

Tracy beckoned her with a finger. "For length, always look at the size of his feet. Big feet . . . that means good length. And for girth, and this is the important part, look at the size and thickness of his index finger. Half an inch from knuckle to knuckle is roughly equivalent to about two inches in girth."

An almost immediate spate of coughing from behind the giant fern almost drowned out Marcel's response. And she gave Tracy a look of exasperation and said, "For God's sake, I can't believe he's still here. Can you tell me why he isn't at home in bed? Coughing and hacking over everyone like that." She clicked her tongue in irritation. "Some people have absolutely no consideration whatsoever."

"Anyway," Tracy said, not paying very much attention to the man or his cough. "So, rule number one is he must be good in bed. And—"

"Rule number one and a half," Marcel said with a little snort of laughter.

Tracy grinned back at her. "I like the way you think. Also, even though he's got to be hung like a horse, he can't be a player. So that's rule number two."

Marcel agreed with great enthusiasm. "Oh, of course not. I would never go for a man like that."

Tracy waved her pen as she got into the spirit of things. "And, rule number three, he has to have some finances. So, that means he has to have a j.o.b."

Marcel wrinkled her nose. "Oh, I wouldn't have it any other way."

"And—wait a minute . . . wait a minute," Tracy said, her voice rising just a little. "This is a good one. He has to have a car. I prefer a foreign model myself. But I'll leave that up to you. And of course, he can't be mean."

Marcel shuddered. "Oh, no. And he has to have his own place."

Tracy squeezed Marcel's arm. "That's right. No men who still live in the basement of their mother's house. And he has to be a loving man, too."

Marcel pressed a hand to her chest. "Oh, I like that. Yes. I really need an affectionate man. One who'll hold my hand when we go shopping in the mall, rub my feet at night . . . and my back. . . ."

Tracy nodded knowingly. "So, what you need is a man with good hands . . . and feet."

"Umm," Marcel agreed. "Nice big feet with capable hands and thick index fingers," she added on a chuckle. "Yes. Now that's what I *need*. And I'm not playing, either."

"Right," Tracy said. "Now we're getting somewhere. This is the kind of man who's bound to keep you happy at home. You know what I mean?"

Both women exchanged a grin.

"You're so right," Marcel said. "But God . . . a man like that, where am I going to find him? Men like that are probably already married or something, you know?"

Tracy rifled around in her handbag again and then emerged with a crisp white business card. She placed it flat on the table.

"This is how you're going to find him," she said.

Marcel looked at the card. "Discreet Singles? A dating agency? Are you out of your mind?"

"It's not just any dating agency," Tracy said, and she tapped the card with a finger. "It's very high-end and very exclusive. They screen their clients carefully. The men are all professionals. Nobody without at least a college degree gets in there. So, we're talking doctors, lawyers, other men like that. They don't even advertise. They don't need to. Women who want quality men go there."

Marcel frowned. "But a dating agency, though? I know I'm thirty years old, but I'm not that desperate yet."

Tracy reached across to grip Marcel's hand. "No, honey, but you do want a man. And this is how you're going to get him."

Ian, listening on the other side of the plant, placed his final forkful of pie in his mouth, reached across to wipe Daniella's mouth, and then pushed back his chair. He had heard enough.

"I'll be right back, Dani. I'm going to have my friend the headwaiter come over and sit with you for just a minute, OK?" he said. "Uncle's got a little matter to take care of."

Chapter Four

Tracy saw him first and the expression on her face caused Marcel to turn in her seat. She bit her tongue hard at the sight of him, and as he approached, her mind went into total panic. What was he doing here? Versailles was one of the most popular eateries in all of San Diego, but still— And why was he walking in their direction? Had he seen her? Did he intend to come across to their table? And if he did come across, what would he say? What did he want? They had said all there was to say to each other already. Unless he'd changed his mind about filing a report with the insurance company. Yes, maybe that was it. He had changed his mind.

"Now, that's what I call a man," Tracy said, leaning forward to touch Marcel on the arm. "And," she stifled a gleeful little sound, "yes, he is. He's coming over."

Marcel met his gaze halfway across the floor and she closed her eyes for half a beat and prayed for strength. She couldn't be weak now. She had the rules. And they did not allow her to consider men like the one who now approached. No players. Absolutely no players.

"Ladies." His voice was a pleasant baritone, and a skitter of heat warmed Marcel's face at the sound of it. Lord, if he wasn't exactly the kind of man she had always dreamed might exist.

Tracy beamed. "Hello there," she said, and then flinched as Marcel's foot made contact with hers beneath the folds of tablecloth.

"Don't be too friendly," Marcel hissed. "He's not on our list of—"

"Shut up," Tracy said, smiling nicely at the approaching man. "He'll hear you."

Ian pulled a chair from a nearby table, placed it neatly beside Marcel, and sat. "I hope you don't mind me coming over for just a minute," and he turned to give Marcel a lazy smile. "Will you introduce me to your friend?"

Marcel swallowed audibly and then said in a dry and cracked manner, "Tracy Roberts. Ian . . . ah. . . ." She tried to remember his name. It ended in an *s*. What was it now? Her brain was in a complete fog. Daniels? Peters? Waters?

"Ian Michaels," he said, leaning forward to give Tracy's hand a very hearty shake. "I'm new in town," he added in a manner that Marcel considered a little too forthcoming.

"Oh, really?" Tracy said, a note of definite interest in her voice. "And how do you know Marcel, then?"

Ian's amber gaze slanted in her direction for a brief instant. "Well, we met only today."

Marcel shot him a sidelong look. He wasn't about to go into all of the sordid details of their meeting, was he? She would never hear the end of it from Tracy if he did. Why didn't he just finish his business with them and leave them to lunch in peace?

But Tracy leaned forward to say with great interest, "Today? When today?"

"I'll tell you later, Tracy," Marcel interrupted. "I'm sure Mr. . . . ah, Michaels—"

"Please call me Ian," he said, cutting neatly into her little speech. And Marcel gritted her teeth at the smooth, dulcet manner in which he did so. She couldn't stand smooth men. Men who always knew what to say in every given situation. They always turned out to be completely untrustworthy in every given situation.

"OK, Ian then," she said grudgingly. "I'm sure Ian doesn't want to rehash all that right now."

Tracy darted a look at Marcel's downturned face and a hint of mischief lit behind her eyes.

"Do you mind if I ask your opinion on a little discussion we've been having, Ian?"

Marcel drew a careful breath and tried in vain to find Tracy's ankle beneath the table. She knew exactly what was about to be said, and for the life of her, she couldn't think of a single way of preventing it.

Ian leaned forward, brushing gently against Marcel's arm as he did. "I'll do what I can to help."

"Tracy . . . this is . . . this is . . ." Marcel struggled to find the right words. But somehow they wouldn't come. It was almost as though English were suddenly completely foreign to her tongue.

Tracy smiled nicely at her and did nothing whatsoever to help her out of her stutter. "Are you a single man, Ian?" she asked instead, not missing a beat.

The dimple in Ian's cheek reappeared, and he nodded and said in a very solemn manner, "I am."

"Good." Tracy nodded, and she avoided the blistering heat of Marcel's eyes. "I need the opinion of someone single."

Marcel made one desperate last-ditch effort to put a halt to the conversation. "Tracy," she said with great urgency, flashing a not-too-subtle glance at her watch, "I have to get back to the office. . . . I've a . . . a . . ." and her throat almost clenched on the lie, ". . . meeting this afternoon. At two-thirty, actually. So, I have to get going. And you should go, too.

Weren't you saying something about an appointment at three?"

Tracy gave her a Cheshire Cat grin and said, "Three o'clock? No, I don't think so. And isn't your two-thirty meeting tomorrow afternoon?" Then, as Marcel wrestled with the repercussions of that, Tracy turned and said to Ian, who was deeply enjoying the interplay between the two women, "Marcel's getting a little forgetful, you know. I always have to remind her when exactly her appointments are. She gets the days mixed up all the time. She thinks it's an age-related problem, but I think . . ."

"Yes?" Ian said, humor flickering in the depths of his amber eyes.

"I think that really, all she needs is a man."

Marcel felt her jaw go slack. She had known that something like this was in the offing, but she had not suspected for a second, not even a second, that Tracy would go this far. She would strangle her. As soon as they were alone again, she would . . . she would . . . Her heart shuddered. *What in the name of heaven was Tracy saying now?* She caught the tail end of another question.

". . . you think of dating agencies?"

Ian leaned back in his chair, and Marcel, who was now almost completely numb, gave Tracy a look of bald horror.

"Well, I have no philosophical problems with using a dating agency, if the situation calls for it. The world has changed a lot over the past ten, twenty years. Both men and women are now heavily involved with their careers. So, finding the time to dive into the dating scene can be a problem for a busy man . . . or woman." And he looked directly at Marcel. And Marcel, in turn, lifted her chin and met his eyes squarely. If he thought she was going to faint from embarrassment, he was going to be sadly mistaken. The initial shock of it all was beginning to ebb, and her ice-cold brain had begun to work once again.

"So, you would use an agency yourself, then?" Marcel widened her eyes and thought at the same time how ridiculous a discussion they were having, and with a complete stranger, too.

"I would." He nodded. "I've a few friends, now married, who met that way."

Marcel's mouth worked. "Well . . . well . . . that's—"

"That's just perfect," Tracy cut in, nodding in a sage manner and earning a wrathful glance from Marcel.

Ian smiled in response and said, "Good. I'm always happy to help whenever I can. And, to that end," and he felt around in the top pocket of his shirt for a little black book. "Can I get your numbers? Being all alone in a new city, it's always nice to have someone to call on. And, you never know, you might be in need of my help again . . . at some point."

Marcel sucked in a breath. What a walking stereotype he was. And that he actually had a *black book* was almost laughable. Well, there was no way under the sun that she was going to do anything remotely social with him. So it didn't matter at all if he had her number. He had quite probably collected hundreds of similar numbers, and all of them that very day. She set her lips firmly, and a brittle little expression settled in her eyes. She didn't have a single second of time for men like Ian Michaels. Not a single second. She had known entirely too many men like him, and she'd had enough of them to last her an entire lifetime. Two lifetimes.

"Here's mine," Tracy said, and she handed Ian one of her nicely embossed business cards. "And Marcel's is . . ." Marcel watched in complete silence as he scribbled her number on the back of Tracy's card. When he was through, he pocketed the card and the black book, cast an unhurried glance at the Discreet Singles business card still lying on the table, scraped back his chair, and stood.

"I'll leave you ladies to finish your lunch."

Although the mere thought of making eye contact with him again made her heart shudder, Marcel met his gaze and forced a smile to her lips. "It's been nice meeting you . . . again," she said. Now, that should show any man of intelligence that she had absolutely no interest in him.

He returned her smile. "We'll be seeing each other again soon."

Marcel nodded and tried her best to keep the smile she didn't feel pinned to her face. He wouldn't be seeing *her* again. That much was certain. The absolute conceit of men like Ian Michaels was astounding. He just assumed that she would have an interest in him. It had probably never even occurred to him that he might not be her type. Well, she would show him a thing or two.

"See you later," Tracy said, waving a cheerful hand at him. Then, as soon as he was out of earshot, she bent low to whisper, "Oh . . . my . . . God. Did you get a look at those fingers? And I think he likes you."

Marcel scraped back her chair. "If we weren't in a public place right now, I'd give you a look at *one* of my fingers."

Tracy gave Marcel the kind of look that didn't fool her for a second. "What? You didn't like him?"

"Telling him, a—a—" Marcel almost gagged on the hot tumble of words, "*total stranger,* that what I really need is a man. What in the name of God could've been going through your head? Have you finally gone completely crazy?"

"But he's interested. You know he's interested.

He probably followed you here to this restaurant somehow just so he could get—"

"Hello? Are you listening to me?" Marcel interrupted. "I don't care if he's interested in me. Were you paying any attention at all to those rules we just came up with? I don't want Ian Michaels. OK? No good-looking men. Read my lips. *No . . . good-looking . . . men.* None. I'm finished with them. Finished. That's all there is to it."

"Well," Tracy said. And Marcel could tell by the expression on her face that she was getting ready to argue the point.

"No," Marcel said. "I mean it." And she bent to retrieve the Discreet Singles business card from the table. "And just to prove to you that I mean what I say, I will go to this . . . this . . ." and she waved the card, "singles place. And, I promise you, the first . . . the very first halfway decent man I run into, if he even comes close to fitting the bill, fitting the rules, he's mine."

Chapter Five

Ian took the coast road after leaving the restaurant and slowed his truck to a crawl so he could admire the glittering blue of the Pacific Ocean.

"Look, Dani," he said, pointing out toward the horizon. "Isn't that a whale out there?"

"A whale? Where? Stop, Uncle. Stop."

Ian pulled the truck over to the side of the road, and for the next several minutes he and his niece watched the curl of the waves together. Six months ago, he had left the child in New York with an aging grandaunt. The plan had been for Daniella to complete the school year there and then join him in California. But Daniella had turned out to be too much of a handful for the old lady. Even when his brother was alive and fully involved in taking care of her, the little girl had shown unusual spurts of temper and a general resistance to most forms of structured discipline. But now, with her father gone, and her mother in and out of various treatment centers, she was almost completely uncontrollable. And none of the distant female relatives had shown any interest at all when asked if they might consider raising the child. In fact, many had bluntly refused to do so. Ian's brow wrinkled. He readily admitted that he knew very little about bringing up a child. Especially a little girl. But, between himself and his house-keeper Vera, a warm and loving home would be pro-vided. The girl would come to understand that she was wanted. And no matter what terrible things she did, she would always be loved.

Ian squinted his eyes against the glare of the set-ting sun. This quiet time was what he had missed. But he would do so no longer. He had made himself a promise a year ago, when his younger brother by just two years had suddenly, and completely without warning, succumbed to a heart attack, that he would not put off living any longer. Long life was clearly not something that was promised to anyone. It had always been his plan to build his business into a strong national conglomerate before considering set-tling into a steady relationship with any one woman. He had thought it unfair to ask anyone to put up with his highly irregular work schedule. Over the past ten years, there had been many days when he had pulled marathon twenty-hour work sessions, just managing to catch a catnap here and there between meetings. He had somehow existed for months on end with no more than two or three hours of sleep a day. He had done it because it had been a necessary sacrifice. It had been the only way to get ahead of the competition. And get ahead he had. He now owned television, radio, and magazine interests. He had been written up favorably in *Money*, *Fortune*, and other such publications, and his company, which was now firmly in control of the East Coast market, was in the process of making an aggressive move across the West Coast territory. He had moved to San Diego to ensure that the company gained a firm foothold in the all-important California market. But that had not been his only reason for shifting his home base from New York. Since his brother's passing, he had begun to feel a strong need for a slower pace of life. He was also getting tired of the parade of women and the hot but meaningless affairs. He wasn't ready to settle down with just one woman or anything like that yet, but he was interested in something a little more . . . stable . . . a little more . . . meaningful. But until he found that, he wasn't opposed to continuing to sample the charms of the fairer sex. He hadn't done nearly enough of that over the past years, and maybe now, before he committed himself to one woman for what would be for him an entire lifetime, he would stop and savor a flower or two. Especially if the flowers were built like Marcel Templeton.

"Ready to go?" he asked Daniella as he reached forward to restart the engine. She nodded her little head in an affirmative and Ian smiled. When he was back in the flow of traffic, he flipped open his cell phone and dialed. She could be sweet natured when she wanted to be.

"Bob," he said as soon as his personal assistant answered. "I'm taking Dani home, then I'll be coming into the office. OK? Let Joe know that I'm gonna want to go over the strategy on that new magazine acquisition. *La Beau Monde*, I think it's called."

Chapter Six

"Good morning," Marcel said brightly as she walked through the tiny reception area and back toward her office. Her assistant, Julie Carter, looked up as she passed and Marcel gave her an expansive smile. She finally felt as though her life was taking a turn for the better. She had spent a good part of last evening thinking about the rules that she and Tracy had come up with. And the more she thought about them, the better she felt about everything. Why she hadn't thought of doing something like this before was completely beyond her. But now she had them, and everything would be fine. She was going to find the perfect man, and together they were going to build a wonderful life. And which woman in her right mind wouldn't be happy about that? In the last twenty-four hours, she had had a major breakthrough. After many years of blundering about in the dark, she finally had a road map that was almost guaranteed to lead her to her dream man.

She set her soft leather briefcase beside her desk, took a quick look at the daily calendar, and then called, "Jules, did you return Tyson Media's call yesterday? What was the name of the guy who called? Joe something-or-other, wasn't it?"

"Joe Mackenzie," Julie said, coming to stand in the doorway. "I spoke to him. He's definitely smooth, I'll give him that. Said he wanted to speak to the owner about a business matter. I tried my best to get it out of him, but . . ."

Marcel sat in the soft leather chair. "That's OK. I'll talk to him. In fact," and she glanced at her watch, "I think I'll give him a call right now. Maybe they're interested in advertising with us. Lord knows we could do with a nice boost to our advertising revenues right about now."

Minutes later, she was being put through to Joe Mackenzie's extension by a very efficient-sounding woman.

"Joe," she said as soon the phone was picked up. "This is Marcel Templeton from *La Beau Monde*."

"Marcel," a deep voice on the other end said. "I've been looking forward to your call."

Marcel's brow wrinkled. She could see what Jules meant about his being smooth. And keen business instinct told her that Joe Mackenzie was not interested in buying advertising space in her magazine.

The complexion of her voice changed by just a shade. "You were looking forward to my call . . . why?"

Joe Mackenzie laughed and then admonished gently, "Now don't sound so suspicious. I promise you, what I have to say to you is going to make your day."

Marcel leaned back in her chair. "Really? And why's that?"

"Well . . . I'd really prefer not to go into the details of this on the phone. But let me just say . . . we're very impressed with what you've done with your magazine. And we'd like to sit down and have a talk with you about direction. The San Diego market is changing. It's becoming a lot more cut-throat. And in a year or two, smaller publications might find it a bit more difficult to survive."

Marcel adjusted the phone against her ear. Now if this didn't just beat everything. But her dad had warned her that this very thing might happen. Tyson Media wasn't the first to show interest in *La Beau Monde*, and chances were, they wouldn't be the last, either. Well, she would just nip this little scheme right in the bud.

"Joe," she said in a pleasant but very firm voice, "I don't want to waste your time, so . . . how can I put this? I have absolutely no interest in selling the magazine. It is a private, family-owned entity, and for as long as I remain the owner and president, it will remain so." Her voice changed and took on an edge of ice. "I hope you understand?"

But it would appear that Joe Mackenzie didn't understand at all. And Marcel was forced to spend the next several minutes rebuffing various invitations to lunch, dinner, and, just before she settled the phone back in its cradle, the opera in New York City. A private all-expenses-paid trip on the corporate jet.

Marcel hung up with the beginnings of a frown in her eyes. She had a strong feeling that this wasn't the end of the matter. But she refused to let it worry her. No matter what enticements Tyson Media threw at her, she was completely firm in her resolve. The magazine was not for sale. And that was all there was to it.

She put the matter completely out of her mind for the remainder of the week, and on Friday evening left the office feeling brightly optimistic.

Chapter Seven

"So . . . all ready for the big date?" Tracy asked, barreling through the half-opened door and almost knocking Marcel over with the mountain of packages in her hands. Marcel beamed happily at her friend. It was a full week since she had paid Discreet Singles a visit, and she was in high spirits because everything had gone so very well. The registration process had been surprisingly painless. She had told them clearly, and without embarrassment, exactly what kind of man she was looking for. And they had assured her very nicely that she had indeed come to the right place if marriage to a man of quality was her primary objective.

"I thought you promised to call me after you got back from the agency. How long ago was that? Two whole weeks." Tracy's voice interrupted Marcel's train of thought.

"A week ago. And I called and left you a message," Marcel said, making a grab for a few of the parcels. "Give me some of those." She closed the door with a shove of her foot and then peered into one of the bulging bags. "What do you have in here? Did you buy the entire store?"

"Just shut up and bring them over here." Tracy collapsed onto a sofa and then bent forward to remove her shoes. "You should be down on your hands and knees thanking me right now." She thrust a foot at Marcel. "Look at that. I know it's going to blister."

Marcel gave the foot an unsympathetic glance. "I told you not to wear those shoes whenever you go on one of your marathon shopping sessions. They're going to end up giving you dragon feet. Remember the girl with the lumpy feet in that movie, ah . . . what's the name again? *Boomerang*?"

Tracy gave her an unconcerned look. "Fine, fine," she said, and then reached forward to proclaim, "Look at this."

She whipped a long and slinky turquoise dress from one of the bags and Marcel covered her mouth and said in a hushed voice, "Oh, my God. That's the dress. That's the one I saw in the window at Saks last week. But it was too expensive. You couldn't have . . ."

Tracy gave her an impish grin and a very pleased "Um-hmm."

"Is it the real thing?"

"Try it on."

Marcel reached out a hand to fondle the fabric. "It feels beautiful. You bought this for me?"

Tracy waved a hand. "This and everything else in these bags."

Marcel's mouth sagged. "No, you didn't."

"Yes, I did."

"Get *out*. You crazy, crazy chick."

Tracy beamed. "Now, what was that you were saying about my marathon shopping sessions and my dragon's feet?"

"I take it back," Marcel said. "Everything I said. I love your shoes, I love your feet." She plucked the dress from Tracy's hands and held it against her body. "There's no way on earth that I won't be able to get a man in *this* dress."

Tracy nodded. "Even J. Edgar Hoover would've been able to get somebody in this dress."

Marcel chuckled. "You're so crazy. I'm going to go try it on." And she made a beeline for the bathroom.

"I got you some shoes to match!" Tracy bellowed at her retreating back. "You know those nice Italian sling backs?"

Marcel was already half out of her clothes by the time she got to the lip of the bathroom door. "You mean the strappy ones with the mesh over the toes?"

"Um-hmm," Tracy confirmed. "But I got you the three-inch heels, not those flat things you were talking about."

Marcel shoved her head out the bathroom door. "You did what?"

"Girl . . . please." Tracy got to her feet and started rooting around in the bags.

Marcel wiggled her hips to properly position the fabric and then yanked on the zipper in the back. "You know I can't walk in anything over two inches," she panted.

She was into the dress now, and it was tight. She spent a moment turning this way and that. Her bosom was perky. But there was no question about it, her butt *was* beginning to sag and her stomach was just too soft. Not flat enough, to be exactly accurate. She could actually see some bulges of cellulite dimpling and smiling hideously at her through the sheen of the cloth.

She squinted at herself in the mirror. It was a nice dress, though. *A very nice dress.* Maybe if she lost ten pounds or so, it might work. She turned around to have a look at the yawn of smooth skin that the elegantly cut back revealed. No red-blooded man in his right mind would be able to ignore her in this dress. Even if she was just a little plumper than the trends of current fashion demanded.

"Finished yet?"

Marcel emerged from the bathroom. It was a little difficult to walk because the dress fit her so very snugly. But she managed it by taking little steps all the way back into the sitting room.

Tracy let out a shriek as soon as Marcel reappeared. "Look at you." She smiled. "I knew I was right. You're gorgeous. Completely gorgeous."

Marcel looked down at the silky fabric. "Girl, do you think it's too tight, though?"

Tracy gave her an incredulous look. "Too tight? What do you mean, too tight?"

"I mean, can't you see the rolls of fat on my stomach?"

Tracy narrowed her eyes. "I don't know what you're talking about. I don't see any rolls of fat anywhere. You don't have a washboard stomach, if that's what you mean. But how many people do?"

Marcel turned sideways and peered at her feet over the swell of her bosom. "It's not that I don't like the dress," she said after a moment. "You know I love it. But I think if I lost some weight, it'd be a great fit."

"Well, you're wearing it in just a couple of hours, so I don't know how you're going to lose any weight by then."

Marcel sucked in her stomach. "What if I wore a corset? What d'you think? It would pull me in and hide all of this," and she gave her stomach a little pat.

Tracy walked around her in a considering circle. "OK," she said after a long moment. "But you've never worn one before, have you? Those things can be tight."

"Don't worry about me," Marcel said, pulling at the bodice of the dress and shifting her bosom into a more favorable position. "Just so long as I don't eat any beans or broccoli between now and then, I'll be fine."

Tracy grinned. "Here. Put the shoes on."

Marcel gave the high-heeled stilettos a dubious look. "If I end up breaking my neck, you know I'm coming back to haunt you. Right?"

Tracy shushed her with a wave of her hand. "You'll be fine. With this kind of dress, you have to." But the rest of what she was about to say was interrupted by the ringing of the phone.

"Grab that for me," Marcel said, balancing herself on one leg as she struggled to get into a shoe.

Tracy picked up the phone and then turned with wide eyes and a hand over the mouth of the handset. "It's him."

The skin between Marcel's brows developed a soft furrow. "Already?" She looked at her watch. "He's too early. I hope he's not on his way over here now."

"Not that one," Tracy said, and she wagged the phone at Marcel. "Ian Michaels. Remember him?"

Marcel shook her head. "Tell him I'm not here. I

don't have the time to talk to him right now, and there's no point to it anyway. I told you that."

Tracy made an exasperated little sound and then spoke nicely into the handset: "She's coming, Ian. . . . No, no, she's not busy. Here she is right now." And she handed over the phone to a stone-faced Marcel.

Marcel grabbed the phone away from her and said in a clipped voice, "Yes, this is Marcel." She listened for a moment and then said in a tone that was not encouraging, "I'm sorry, but that won't be possible. I'm getting ready for a date right now. And no, later on this evening wouldn't work, either. But thank you for thinking of me. Have a nice evening."

"Are you crazy?" Tracy asked as soon as Marcel hung up. "Are you seriously going to pass up a man like that when it's so obvious that he wants you?"

Marcel shoved her foot into the other shoe. "Does he fit in with my rules? Can't you tell he's not looking for anything serious . . . that he's a player?" She lifted her eyebrows, emphasizing the question.

"Sometimes you have to be willing to—"

"That's not the issue," Marcel interrupted. "Does he or does he not fit into the guidelines that both you and I agreed to?"

Tracy mumbled something heated beneath her breath, and Marcel asked, "What was that?"

"Never mind."

"That's right," Marcel said, nodding her head.

"He doesn't fit. You know he doesn't fit. I know he doesn't fit. So, what am I spending time with him for? I don't have time to waste. And Ian Michaels, as fine as he is, is just not the kind of man that I want to date . . . let alone marry. OK? He's probably a . . . a gigolo or something. Could a man like that help me save my dad's magazine? Would he even understand or care about why I have to do that? I mean, he's probably got the basic intelligence to grasp the intricacies of the magazine business, but do you really think that he'd want to? I need a partner, you know what I mean? Not just someone who looks good."

"OK. Fine," Tracy said. "I just hope that the man who shows up this evening is the kind you think you want. That's all. Because I'm really sick and tired of going through this with you. You're such a pain."

Marcel ignored that and instead gave her right foot a wiggle. "I saw a videotape of him, and he's exactly what I'm looking for, looks-wise. So, I don't think I'll have to worry too much about him and other women, because they just won't want him."

Tracy made a noncommittal sound and then said with some amount of irritation in her voice, "What are you doing to that shoe?"

Marcel looked down at the shoe that she was still attempting to shove her foot into. "I'm telling you, I don't think I can spend an entire evening in these shoes. They're too high for me. My ankles feel like they're going to buckle."

Tracy got down on her knees and grabbed ahold of Marcel's right foot. "You didn't do the straps right. They're supposed to give you support, not cut off your circulation." She yanked a strap loose and then with practiced hands laced everything up again. "There," she said after several minutes of pulling and yanking. "Now, that's what they're supposed to look like." And she straightened from her crouch. "You've got pretty feet, but it's gonna take much more than just that to get this husband you say you want. You have to do some serious work on some other areas, or no man, I don't care what he looks like, is gonna stay with you."

"What're you trying to say?" Marcel asked, putting her hands on her hips. "You think I have personality problems?"

Tracy pursed her lips. "You have issues."

Marcel made a disgusted sound. "I don't have issues."

"Right," Tracy said. "Remember, this is me you're talking to, not some stranger off the street. You know and I know that you have issues with men. That's why—" And she held up a hand as Marcel drew breath to interrupt. "That's why you always end up choosing the wrong one."

Marcel's mouth sagged open. "Where is this coming from? You've never said any of this to me before. You know it hasn't been my fault that things haven't worked out with any of the men I've dated. You know that."

Tracy sighed. "You can't take criticism for one, *that* I know. But sometimes you really need to hear it."

Marcel's chin tilted and her eyes took on a defiant sparkle. "It's not criticism that I can't take," and she struggled for a moment to find the right words. "I just can't believe that you would say something like that. I mean why . . . how could you say that when you know . . . you know what I've been through?"

They faced each other across the small expanse of carpet and their eyes battled for an instant. But Tracy refused to back down this time.

"It's true. You're carrying around some baggage. And I've been meaning to talk to you about it for a while now. But you know what you're like. This whole thing with Ian Michaels, though . . ." And she propped a hand on her hip. "I just couldn't let it go this time."

Marcel shook her head. "You're so typical. You know that the only reason you like Ian Michaels is because you've fallen for his whole 'Look at me, I'm such a *nice* guy' routine." She rolled her eyes. "Can't you tell that it's just an act? God, I know on a scale from one to ten, he's probably a twelve in the looks department, but really now, there's much more to life than just looks, Tracy, I keep telling you that. Don't be so shallow, for God's sake."

Tracy's eyes widened. "Shallow? You're accusing *me* of being shallow? Are you the same person who couldn't bear to date a man under six feet? Or the one who told me that any man who couldn't afford to buy you a house wasn't one you would ever give any time—"

"That was years ago. I've matured a lot since then," Marcel cut her off. "You know," and she waved an exasperated hand, "you never understand what I'm talking about, and you always have something stupid to say. I don't know why I even bother to tell you anything." She bent to pick up the shoes. "Anyway," she continued. "I'm not talking about this now. I have to go get ready before my date shows up."

Tracy picked up two of the shopping bags and followed her back to the bedroom. "There's no point in being mad at me, either. If I don't tell you these things . . . who will?"

Marcel tossed her a look over her shoulder. "I'm not mad at you."

"Right. And that's why you've got that evil look on your face."

A hint of a smile trembled about Marcel's lips. "You get on my last nerve, you know that? Help me get my makeup out. And my black ultrasheer panty hose."

Tracy dumped the bags on the large four-poster bed. "I got some more stuff in here for you. A black spiderweb dress that you definitely won't wear until you think he . . . whoever that turns out to be . . . is trembling on the brink of a serious proposal. And . . ." She paused to root around in another bag. "A couple other things you're definitely going to need. And some more shoes. . . ." Her eyes grew pensive. "No corset, though."

"Shoot," Marcel said, poking her head around the bathroom door. "And I know I don't have anything like that. Can you go get one for me?"

"What?" Tracy said. "After calling me stupid and shallow, you want me to go do something else for you?"

"Come on," Marcel coaxed. "I'll name my first child after you . . . boy or girl!"

"I want you to know that I don't love you right now."

Marcel turned on the shower and bellowed above the downpour, "Yes, you do! You love me! With all my issues and baggage and everything! You love me to death!"

Tracy muttered something Marcel didn't hear, and then said over the sound of the running water, "I'm taking your keys. You'd better be finished in there by the time I get back."

At the slam of the outer door, Marcel popped back under the shower. She turned the tap to steaming hot and stood with her eyes closed as the needles of water hit her skin. If the man who showed up tonight was even halfway decent she was going to go after him like she had never gone after a man before. He was a banker or stockbroker or somebody like that. Exactly the kind of financial man she needed to help her run the magazine. She had made her father a promise on his deathbed that she would turn the family magazine into the kind of business enterprise that he was never able to make it during his lifetime. And she was determined to keep that promise. So Ian Michaels would do well to put his lascivious plans for her on hold, because nothing he said or did would have any effect whatsoever. Absolutely none. And even if he stepped up the pressure and she felt herself getting weak, it still wouldn't work. She had her rules to make her strong. And strong she would be. Strong she would be.

Chapter Eight

Ian sat out on the whitewashed balcony, his legs propped comfortably against the thick wraparound banister. Just below, the waves foamed lazily on the sand. And out toward the golden horizon, the burnt orange sun sank slowly toward the sea.

"Dani?" he called as a sound from within the child's bedroom caught his attention.

"Yes, Uncle Ian?"

"Are you in bed?"

"But, Uncle, it's still early. Do I have to?"

"Yes, you do, young lady," he said with just the right degree of firmness in his voice. "I'll be in to read you a story in just a little while, OK?"

"OK," the child said with the beginnings of heat in her voice.

Ian smiled and pushed a thick curl out of his eyes.

He had two very strong-willed females in his life now. His niece and Marcel Templeton. It had been a long while since a woman, any woman, had caused him to reflect this much. And it bothered him. Not for any of the traditional reasons, of course. He had never placed much stock in his particular brand of looks. In fact, he hardly acknowledged them at all. So he was constantly surprised that so much was often made of them. What did trouble him, though, was the fact that Marcel Templeton appeared to very genuinely not like him at all. He was well accustomed to not being appreciated in business-related situations, but he had always been a tremendous success in the social arena. He had never had to try that hard, though. Most women had been more than flattered by his attentions. But Marcel Templeton was a different kettle of fish. She appeared almost insulted by them. He had not really taken her *rules* that seriously at the restaurant, but it would appear that she had not been joking.

A frown appeared between his brows, and he reached for the silver tray at his side. He polished the smooth surface free of residual water droplets and then glared at his reflection. After a moment he replaced the tray and called for Vera, his housekeeper. A matronly woman appeared just moments later, wiping her hands hastily on the colorful apron hanging from about her waist.

"Tell me the truth, Vera, and don't spare my feelings," he said without preamble. "How would you describe me?"

"Describe you, honey?" the woman asked, confusion shining brightly for a moment in her eyes.

"Yes, you know what I mean," Ian said. "How do I look to you?"

"Oh." Vera nodded. And she peered with great concern at her employer's face. "You're not feeling well." She ran a motherly hand across his brow. "I've been telling you for months now that you have to take it easy. Look at what happened to your brother. You can't work yourself to death. Having a good business is fine, but not if it means killing yourself at a young age."

Ian held the leathery hand in his and pressed a kiss to the chapped back of it. "I feel fine. What I want to know is, do you think I'm good-looking?"

The housekeeper pulled her hand from his. "Good-looking? You?" And she threw her head back and laughed in a very hearty manner. "God be praised," she said after the spasm had passed. "You've never been concerned about that before. What's brought this on?" Then she nodded knowingly and gave an "Ah. So, she doesn't think you're attractive enough for her?"

Ian grimaced. "I'm beginning to think I might be too attractive. She seems to want a man who—"

"Doesn't have gold eyes and curly black hair," Vera interrupted. "Well, leave her be then. She's probably not worth the trouble. If that's all she can see," and the housekeeper shrugged, "there's nothing you can do."

"I could change her mind," Ian said.

"You like her that much?"

Ian squinted out at the water. "She's . . . different." He turned and looked at the woman who had been as close to him as a mother. A sudden smile softened the severity of his face. "She's interesting. I can't explain it. I don't know what it is. Maybe it's *because* she doesn't like me."

The housekeeper propped her hands on her ample hips. "Well, you'll sort it out. You always do."

Ian smiled. Yes. He would sort it out.

Chapter Nine

"Oh, my God," Tracy said, turning away from the window. "I think he's here. And would you look at that car?"

Marcel eased herself off the stool and walked as quickly as the stiletto heels would allow across to the window. Her eyes fell immediately on a beautiful red sports model.

She drew a steadying breath. Suddenly she wasn't completely sure that she was doing the right thing. "That's him."

Tracy craned her neck. "What kind of car is it?" she asked, turning to give Marcel a diamond-bright look.

"A Lamborghini, I think."

Tracy's eyebrows lifted. "A Lamborghini? Isn't that one of those really expensive Italian cars?"

"Um-hmm," Marcel agreed. "But where is he? Did you see him get out?"

"Maybe he's—" But before Tracy could finish her thought, the phone began to ring.

Marcel snatched it up. "Hello?" She nodded at Tracy and then said in a very pleasant manner, "OK. I'll be right down."

"He's not coming up?" Tracy asked as soon as Marcel had hung up the phone.

Marcel gathered up her bag. "He said he doesn't want to leave his car alone in this neighborhood. He wants me to come down."

"Well, you know how these rich guys are, honey," Tracy said in a consoling manner. "They're accustomed to having everything their way. But it'll be fine. It'll be fine," and she hustled Marcel toward the door. "Just remember, don't make it too easy for him now. Make him work for it."

Marcel straightened the fall of her skirt. "I'm OK? My hair, makeup, everything?"

Tracy gave her a brief kiss on the side of the face and shoved her out the front door. "You're beautiful. I'll be here until you get back. Now, go and get that man."

Marcel swallowed away the nervous dryness in the back of her throat as the front door closed behind her. This was it. This was it. But she had to be cool like Tracy had said. Friendly but not overanxious. Pleasant but not too quick to please. She had to be witty and intelligent. She had to feel him out. See what his interests were. Maybe he was the kind of guy who liked to talk politics or sports. In both areas she was unsurpassed. So she would be able to dazzle him with her brilliance and wide breadth of knowledge.

"Marcel!" her closest neighbor from across the hedge called almost as soon as she stepped onto the gravel path. "You look lovely this evening."

Marcel thanked the elderly man nicely and returned his greeting with a bright smile. Her expression faltered a bit as she approached the car. She might look like she was well put together, but she certainly didn't feel it. Her underwear was beginning to ride up on her, and the corset that Tracy had strapped so very snugly to her body was squeezing her so tightly that she could barely breathe.

She walked down the short gravel path and into the soft evening breeze. Her eyes went immediately to the red sports model and to the man who was in the process of squeezing his rather large bulk from behind the wheel.

Her eyes flashed over him. Yes, this was exactly the man she had seen in the video. He was of medium height, possessed a soft pot belly, and appeared to be suffering from a peculiar form of random balding. She squinted at him. He also seemed to have lost quite a lot of hair since the taping of his video message.

But it didn't matter. What was a little hair, after all? So what if his head resembled that of a parrot with a bad case of molt? Such a minor thing wasn't at all significant in the bigger scheme of things. This was exactly the kind of man who would be good to her. He had solid, dependable features. He had the look of a family-oriented man. And this was a good sign. Family men were unlikely to suddenly start lying and sneaking around with an entire horde of women as soon as her back was turned. Family men were responsible, dependable, and, most of all, loving and affectionate.

The man in question beamed at her as she got closer, and Marcel tried her best not to stare at the strange tufts of hair that appeared to be barely clinging to his skull.

"Marcel?"

"Yes." She smiled. "And you must be Bill?"

"That's right." He nodded. "Bill Cook, live and in living color." And he walked around to swing open the passenger side door.

"Oh," Marcel said, and there was a pleased note in her voice. "Thank you. You're so polite." And she clambered into the low leather interior of the car. Even though he was about an hour late and had offered her no apology or explanation, she could forgive him because it was clear that he was a man with good manners.

Bill gave her an especially wide grin as soon as she was properly seated, and then leaned forward to whisper in a conspiratorial manner, "Can I give you a hug?"

Marcel blinked. "A hug?" What was this now?

"You know, just to jump things off right."

She rested her handbag on the seat while her mind went quickly through the options. It would be best not to appear too standoffish. She didn't want him to think that she wasn't a warm person. "Sure. But make it a quick one."

And before she could even utter another word, he reached forward and dragged her close, flattening his body against hers.

"You know," he muttered, bending his head to sniff the crevice between her neck and shoulder, "you're exactly the kind of woman I like to hold. So damn thick and juicy. I'd like to just chew on one of those legs." And he rubbed his nose against her earlobe and grunted, "We're going to have a *good* time tonight."

Marcel took a breath as he released her. There was no need to panic. He was probably just eccentric. Most wealthy men were known to be a little strange. But, just in case, she would keep her index finger on the nozzle of her can of Mace. A sharp blast of that would soon cure him of whatever pe-

culiarities ailed him. Her brow furrowed just a bit.
She was being too hasty, though. The evening, after
all, had only just begun.

She arranged herself in the deep leather seats and
waited as he settled himself behind the wheel and
then turned the key in the ignition. The engine
roared to life.

"Like my car?" he asked above the noise of the
motor.

"It's—" But before she could even complete her
thought, he flung the car into gear and shot down
the driveway in reverse. The movement was so unexpected that Marcel very nearly bit the tip off of
her tongue. Her hands went automatically to check
that her seat belt was securely fastened.

He noticed the furtive activity of her hands and
sought to reassure her with an "It's OK, baby.
You're all right with me."

Marcel gave him a simmering look. "You must
get a lot of tickets if you drive like this all the time."

Bill laughed. "Tickets. Right. They've gotta catch
me first, baby." And he patted the soft leather steering wheel. "This is my girl. She's the kind of woman
who'll never let me down, you know what I mean?"

Marcel gritted her teeth and turned to stare out
the window. Well, it certainly looked as though this
date was not going to work out. Why in the name
of heaven couldn't she ever find a normal man?
Were they all completely out of their minds? Or did

the universe just have it in for her in particular?

"Where're we going?" she asked after a long moment of silence. And her gaze flickered across the steadily rising speedometer needle and then back to the face of the man seated beside her.

He leaned over to touch her on the leg. "I know this nice little place in downtown San Diego. Exclusive little joint. It's got good food, and even better music. Only the cool people are allowed, though. Are you cool, Marcel?" And he took a corner at sixty miles per hour and then headed for the freeway in a fresh burst of speed.

"Look," Marcel said as soon as they had blended safely with the evening traffic. "I think you'd better slow down."

Bill looked across at her and winked. "Slow down? This girl was built for speed, honey. You know what I'm saying?"

Marcel pursed her lips. "I know what you're saying, but the question is, do you know what *I'm* saying?"

He shot her a sidelong little look. "Relax, baby. Don't be so uptight. You want to have some fun tonight, right? That's why we're both in this thing. Am I right? Or am I right?"

Marcel felt the blood begin its slow but inevitable rise toward her head. She closed her eyes for a second and prayed for control.

"Don't tell me you're one of those church girls,

baby?" And he swore in a thick and completely un-restrained manner. "It's getting so that a man can't catch a break these days."

Marcel's eyes snapped back open, and her hands tightened in her lap. Well, she had tried. She had re-ally, really tried. But, rules or no rules, this was it. She had had just about enough. More than enough.

"Are you on any medication or anything?" She was through with being polite.

"Medication?" he bellowed. "I'm all natural, baby. All natural." He changed lanes in a swooping motion and then accelerated to ninety.

Marcel twisted in her seat to look at the stream of traffic behind them. When she addressed him again, her voice held the kind of calm that warned of an explosion to come.

"I think there's a motorcycle cop somewhere be-hind us."

Bill adjusted himself with a hand and grunted, "You're bringing me down, baby. You're bringing me down."

Marcel's eyes darted to the speedometer again. It was now reading exactly 100 miles per hour. She nodded to no one in particular and muttered beneath her breath. If he didn't slow the car down, and soon, it was more likely than not that she would be beating him down in only seconds.

"You'd better slow down. I'm telling you, we just passed a CHP cop."

Bill made a snorting little noise. "A cop? On a bike? Don't worry, we can outrun him. Watch this." And he floored the gas pedal.

Marcel held on to her pocketbook. God help her, she was in the car of a complete lunatic. A madman. And to make matters worse, it felt as though her underwear had finally decided on which position it liked best. The soft and satiny band of fabric that had appeared so eye-catching just a few hours earlier had now retreated to lodge very firmly somewhere between the base of her spine and the middle of her brain.

She wiggled in a futile attempt to gain some relief and then resigned herself to the discomfort of it. What was a little cloth at a time like this? She had much more important things to consider, staying alive being the most pressing concern.

As the car whistled along, she gripped both sides of the seat and pondered her fate in an almost abstract manner. How in the name of God did she always manage to get herself into situations like these? If she got out of this one alive, though, that agency was going to feel the full force of her tongue. What could possibly have possessed them to send her on a date with a man like Bill Cook? Sure, she had been the one to choose him, but she had naturally assumed that all of their clients were sane.

The car swooped to the right, the left, and then, just as she had suspected would happen, there was the sudden wail of sirens behind them. She squeaked an eye open and shrieked, "What do you think you're doing? You can't possibly outrun them."

Bill grinned at her. "Don't worry, I've done this before. Besides . . . the chief of police is a friend of mine. It's a little game we play. They won't touch me."

Marcel turned again to look and her heart shuddered. Where had all of those other black-and-whites suddenly come from? Jesus God Almighty, she and Bill were now involved in a full-scale police pursuit. They were going to jail for sure. Better yet, with the way things were going for her of late, she would probably be the one to end up in the slammer. They were going to take her straight to the big house. Even though none of it had been her doing. Even though all she had wanted to do was find a husband. It was karma or something. Maybe she'd been a very evil person in another life and now she was paying for it.

She reached a hand for the hefty pocketbook in her lap. Karma or not, though, she wasn't going down without a struggle; that much was certain. She would beat Bill Cook senseless if necessary.

"Pull this car over right now," she said, "or I swear to God, I'll . . ." And she lifted her very sizable handbag.

Bill's eyes darted across her face and then dipped to the bag in her hand. And something about the lack of expression on her face alerted him to the seriousness of the situation.

"Aren't you having any fun, baby? You sure you want me to stop?"

Marcel's brow creased. Fun? He actually thought that this was fun? Being chased down the freeway by a horde of cops? He was definitely insane.

She drew a tight breath and released it. "Stop the car. Now." If they were really lucky, she might be able to talk her way out of the current situation.

Bill muttered something that Marcel paid absolutely no attention to. Her eyes were trained on the circle of police cars that seemed to be growing larger by the second. And, as the car slowed, her mind raced through a myriad of possible explanations. She could say she had been kidnapped. No. They wouldn't believe that one. OK. Maybe she could tell them that the man behind the wheel had suffered a sudden nervous breakdown. Why not? People succumbed to sudden heart attacks, didn't they? Why not sudden nervous breakdowns? It could happen. It could. Or she could try the truth, of course. She could tell them that she had never met this . . . this Bill Cook person before. That she was on a kind of blind date with a man who was clearly dealing with some very serious mental issues. But who would believe that? They would think that she had encouraged him in some way. They would laugh her to scorn. They would send her to jail.

She blinked eyes that had suddenly gone bone-dry. Great. Just great. That was all she needed now.

Her contacts were beginning to act up. What more was going to happen to her? What more?

As soon as the car came to a complete stop on the shoulder of the highway, they were hemmed in by a swarm of squad cars.

What ensued over the next several minutes was something that Marcel would not soon forget. They were both forced from the car, despite the grand protestations of her date as to the important people whom he knew personally. Then they were made to face the hood, with arms and legs spread, while at least six policemen went over the entire vehicle with various pieces of electronic equipment. Marcel was then, to her chagrin, subjected to a complete body search, during which she somehow managed to break her shoe heel on a large piece of gravel, lose her right contact lens, and completely ruin her nicely coiffed hair.

At the end of it all, Bill was given a hefty fine and she, with one eye now closed against the tearing wind, was told that she was old enough to know better and that she should definitely make use of better judgment in the future.

And, just as she was beginning to think that maybe the worst of the entire affair was over, she caught sight of a familiar white truck in the maze of vehicles going slowly by the spectacle on the shoulder of the road.

Chapter Ten

Marcel blinked her good eye and tried to focus on the truck. It couldn't be true. It just could not be happening. What was Ian Michaels doing on this particular freeway? At this particular time of day? Hadn't she just spoken to him an hour ago? Was he following her?

She discarded the possibility of that almost as soon as it occurred. No, that was ridiculous. Why would he be following her? He probably had much better things to do with his time than follow her around. Especially when he knew that there was absolutely no point to it anyway.

She tried not to look at the white truck as it went slowly by. Maybe he hadn't seen her. Or better yet, maybe he wouldn't recognize her. She was a mess, after all. One of her eyes was squinted shut because of the loss of the contact lens. The other was red and her hair was standing up around her head like a windblown hay basket. Why should he recognize her? Of course he wouldn't. There was no chance of that.

She watched the truck with her good eye slitted against the wind. Oh lord. He was going to stop. He *had* seen her. He was pulling over onto the shoulder of the road just up ahead. Getting out. Oh, no.

She gave her dress and broken shoe a hurried glance. This was truly the worst day of her life. God Almighty. And her idiotic date was still attempting to argue his way out of the ticket. What a mess. What an absolute—

"Hello. Need some help?"

His voice caused the baby-fine hairs at the nape of her neck to stand at rigid attention, and Marcel stood firmly on the thrill that warmed her. Why did he have to possess that kind of voice? Why was fate doing this to her?

"Hi," and a million and one possible responses flashed through her head. And in the fractional amount of time that it took to sort through them all, she decided to brazen things out. This entire incident had not been her doing anyway, so why should she feel ashamed or embarrassed? If anyone should be embarrassed at all, it was the crazy man who was still in the process of arguing with the ticketing officer.

She faced Ian squarely, not caring a bit that his eyes were now trained on her broken shoe.

"Would you mind giving me a lift back home? If it's not too much trouble?" Her voice was crisp, clear, and she made her request without so much as a tremor in her voice. If he had not shown up just then, she would have asked one of the officers to take her back home. Because there was no way on earth that she was getting back into Bill Cook's car. So Ian Michaels could either refuse to take her home because of the rude manner in which she had treated him before, or take pity on her and help her out of her predicament.

A smile flickered for an instant in his eyes, and the puzzling dimple in his cheek presented itself. Marcel gave her chin a little tilt. Let him laugh then; it didn't matter that he found her predicament amusing. It was what she expected from a man like him. He had probably never experienced a single sympathetic emotion in his entire self-indulgent life.

"Go and sit in the truck," Ian said, handing her the small bunch of keys in his hand. "I'll straighten things out here."

Marcel accepted the keys without argument, limped her way to the battered old truck, wrenched open the passenger door, and clambered in. Maybe she should just give up on men altogether. She could maybe find herself a nice little convent and live out the remainder of her days there in peace. She sighed.

But of course that was a complete fantasy. And even her rules, as good as they were, couldn't protect her from the Bill Cooks of the world.

Marcel turned as the truck door opened. She was instantly on guard again.

"I think you made the right decision."

Her eyebrows lifted. "I'm sorry . . . what?"

"I think you made the right decision about ending your date with . . ." And he spread his fingers in a completely male gesture.

"Bill," Marcel said, resigned.

He gave her a sidelong glance and then said smoothly, "Yes. Bill. He seems to be hell-bent on arguing his way into even deeper trouble. You were wise to discontinue the evening's festivities. I'm glad I came along when I did. It's not the kind of situation that a woman like you should be in."

She let that particular comment pass and said, "Thank you very much for stopping. I would've asked one of the officers to take me home, but I am, ah . . . grateful that you agreed. I hope this doesn't take you too far out of your way?"

He leaned a little too close for Marcel's comfort, changed gears smoothly, and then said with a husky edge to his voice, "I was actually on my way to the movies. Thought I might grab something to eat along the way. Would you like to join me, since your dinner plans have been ruined? You must be getting hungry."

Marcel blinked. Lord, but he was smooth. She hadn't even seen that one coming.

"I'm not dressed for the movies," she said after giving her choice of words some thought. "Besides, after what I've just been through, I really just want to go home, have a shower, and go straight to bed."

"OK," he said, and there was no trace of pique in his voice. "But don't let this unfortunate incident make you give up hope . . . ah, give up dating. Not all men are like . . . Bill."

Marcel pursed her lips in an unconscious little tightening of her mouth. Five months ago, she would have swallowed his little sympathy routine hook, line, and sinker. But a lot of water had passed under the bridge since then. She felt like an experienced woman now. No longer wet behind the ears. She didn't believe in ridiculous dreams anymore. This was the real world. So there was absolutely no point to his little routine. It would have no effect whatsoever. None. And the sooner he realized it, the better it would be for him. He would be able to change directions and begin his pursuit of more interesting prey.

"I know that Tracy managed to give you the impression the other day that . . . that I'm in some kind of desperate search for a man," she began now with rapidly mounting ire. "But I'm not. OK? So you can just stop hitting on me. I'm not some chick who's going to fall for your smooth lines. So, let's just—"

"Of course you aren't," he said, cutting her off very neatly. "You're obviously a very beautiful and intelligent woman."

Marcel stared at him. "What?" She had not expected that kind of response from him. Why didn't he react the way she wanted? She had lashed out at him. Why did he not respond in kind? Why didn't he say that she was an ungrateful harpy who, if she didn't look sharp, would find herself old and alone without anybody at all to love?

"You are a beautiful and intelligent woman," he said again. "But of course, I'm not telling you anything that you don't already know."

"Look," she said, somewhat wearily. "I don't know how to say this politely, so I'm just going to come out and say it. I am not interested in any of your flattery. So, you can just give it up, OK?" She turned toward the window and tried not to think about how badly she was behaving.

They drove for the next few minutes in complete silence, and then he surprised her by asking, "What is it about me that you dislike so much?"

Marcel turned toward him in surprise. "Dislike you? I don't even know you."

"Exactly," he agreed. And he swept the old truck into the slow lane. "You don't know me, and yet you very obviously do not care for me at all. So, tell me, what is it? You seem like a nice woman. I'm a fairly decent sort of guy. With these two things going for us, we should be able to at least talk to each other, shouldn't we?"

Marcel scraped a hand through her hair and succeeded in making an even greater mess of it. She was definitely not going there with him. She just wanted to go home.

"Take the next exit," she said.

He did as she instructed, and then said, "So you're not going to answer my question?"

Marcel tightened her lips, relaxed them, and then tightened them again. OK. Fine. She'd just have to be blunt about it.

"If you want to know the truth," she began.

"I do." He nodded.

She ignored the nice tone in his voice. "I don't . . . care for men like you. You're all completely the same. You may look different, wear different clothes, different shoes, drive different cars, but essentially, you're all exactly the same man. And how men like you tend to treat women is nothing to be proud of. Turn here."

He turned with a smooth sweep of the wheel. "So, you really think you've got me all figured out, then?"

"There's nothing much to figure out. You're completely transparent to me."

He actually chuckled at that, and Marcel gave him

a hard little look. He could laugh about it if he liked, but she was entirely certain that the many women whose hearts he had broken would not be similarly amused.

"And you've based this completely damning analysis of me on just the way I look?"

Marcel gave him a superior smile. "I'm a very good judge of people," she said, and blinked rapidly as she remembered that it was she who had chosen to go out with the lunatic Bill Cook. And she who had gotten caught up with Alex. "Well, I usually am . . . that is."

Ian smiled, and Marcel's traitorous heart fluttered in response. "Well, in this case, I think you may have gotten your signals a little crossed."

"I really don't think so."

"So, what does this mean? Are you saying that we can't be friends?"

Marcel sighed. "I'm sure you don't really need my friendship. I know you have more female friends than you can handle without adding me to the collection."

This earned her a guffaw and Marcel gave an offended sniff. He was really the most irritating person. Any normal man would have left her on the side of the road in a magnificent display of male pride.

"Regardless of the number of friends I currently have, I'd still like to count you as one. So, what do you think? Will you bury the hatchet? Be my friend?"

"It's the last house on the right," Marcel said. Thank the lord she was almost home. She couldn't take very much more of this particular onslaught. It was beginning to severely tax her nerves. No matter what she threw at him, he continued to respond to her with good humor.

"OK, fine. I can't see how it'll serve you, but OK, I'll be your friend." She hoped that agreeing to this nonsensical friendship business would shut him up.

"Good." And his smile was so irritatingly warm that Marcel turned her gaze away. He had entirely too much charisma for his own good.

"You can just drop me off here. You don't have to bother to drive all the way in."

"Leave you at the head of your driveway, at this time of night? What kind of friend would do that?"

A reluctant smile flickered about Marcel's lips. He had outplayed her with one simple stroke. How interesting.

She turned speculative eyes toward him and almost shuddered as her gaze sank deep into his beautiful amber-gold eyes. Maybe there was more to him than she had thought. Lord, if he really possessed a better than average brain beneath all that beauty . . .

"OK, if it's not too much trouble. But I have to warn you, I can't invite you in. I'm in no shape to entertain right now."

His eyes flickered over her in an almost imperceptible movement.

"You look fine to me."

Marcel kept silent. Of course he would say that. She had expected it as soon as she put the comment out there.

"Your grass needs to be cut," he said as the truck rolled to a stop on the gravel.

"Yes. I know," she agreed. There were a lot of things that needed attention around the house. There were broken pipes, clogged guttering, and shabby paintwork, as well as any number of other little problems. But they would all have to wait until she could afford to hire a team of contractors to do the work.

"Thank you very much for rescuing me back there," she said now. "And . . . and I'm sorry if I said anything to offend you. Sometimes my mouth gets the better of me."

"It's much better to be honest about your feelings than to bottle everything up. Now we both understand each other a little better. That's the important thing." He touched her lightly on the arm and Marcel's eyes went to dwell with almost hypnotic fascination on the girth of his index finger. A bead of sweat appeared above her lip. Lord, Tracy should not have revealed that magical connection between thickness of finger and size of equipment.

Marcel raised hot eyes. Lord, but he had big

hands, though . . . and feet. If Tracy was right about her little formula . . .

"Yes, well," she said, "I'll see you then." She scrabbled for the door handle.

"Just a minute."

And before she could even guess at what it was he intended, he was out of the truck and opening the door for her.

She swallowed. What strange gentlemanly behavior for a player.

"Thank you." And her voice held bemused surprise as his hand settled beneath her elbow. He helped her down from the truck, waited for her to properly regain her balance, and then said, "I'm sorry things didn't work out tonight."

Marcel nodded. She couldn't take very much more of this. "And I'm sorry about ruining your . . . movie and dinner."

He shrugged. "I've had a much better time with you." And he ran a quick finger down the side of her cheek.

Marcel held her breath as he did and repeated silently, *He's just playing with me. He's just playing with me.*

When she said nothing in reply, he stepped back and said, "I'll wait in the truck until you go inside."

Less than two minutes later, Marcel was opening her front door to Tracy's horrified, "Oh, my God. What happened to you?"

Chapter Eleven

It took a full hour of explaining before Tracy had completely grasped the enormity of what had transpired on the ninety-minute date from hell. And another half an hour before the corset Marcel had been strapped into was properly removed and the offending piece of silk underwear torn to shreds and then tossed into the trash compactor. Fifty dollars literally down the drain.

At the end of the evening, after she had reassured Tracy repeatedly that she was definitely going to be fine, and that she didn't have to spend the night, Marcel wrapped herself in an old terry cloth bathrobe and hunkered down before the TV set in the living room with an appropriately large tub of rocky road ice cream. She ate the entire thing while flipping aimlessly through a variety of half-hour sitcoms. And very soon everything became a blur. Two girlfriends living in Minnesota—their lives were just as messed up as hers. A black-and-white show about a TV writer and his perfect sixties wife. Perfect. She snorted and continued to flip through the channels. A high-octane cop show set in Miami. A black cop. A white cop. Beautiful lives. Beautiful people. Everything there was beautiful. Maybe she should hire someone to run the magazine, move there, set up a shack on the beach, and sell things she found in the sand. Tourists would buy them. They'd buy anything as long as it was all strung together on a chain. And that couldn't be any worse than what she was doing now in San Diego.

Marcel wandered aimlessly from station to station, pausing for a moment to absorb the story line, and then continuing her journey through cable land. Her brain felt completely frozen, and she wasn't sure whether it felt that way because of the rising tide of fear that was somewhere just below the pit of her stomach or because of all the ice cream she had just consumed.

She was right in the middle of watching the usual parade of freaks on the *Howard Stern* show when the phone rang. She cast a malevolent glare at the instrument, wiped the corner of her mouth with a napkin, and uttered a silent prayer, *Please, God, let it not be Ian Michaels.* She'd had more than enough of his little act for one evening.

"Hello?" She wasn't going to talk to him for any length of time, if it was him. She had already said her thank-yous twice, so what more could she say? Was he brain-damaged or something? And if he started off with the entire friendship nonsense again, she would just have to hang up.

"Hi, honey." *Oh God.* Her mother. She couldn't take anything more. Not yet. Not so soon.

"Hi, Mom. I was going to give you a call tomorrow."

Her mother ignored her. "You know, Marcy, I've been thinking."

Marcel's throat went dry. It was always a bad sign when her mother started off with that particular opening comment.

"What have you been thinking?"

"Well . . . and I know you've been trying your best, dear heart, but I was thinking that maybe the reason you don't have a man yet is because you don't try hard enough in the right way—"

"But, Mom, I'm—"

"No, honey," her mother said, cutting her off. "This time you're going to listen to me."

Marcel rolled her eyes. When did she ever not listen to her? All she ever did was listen to her.

"You're too self-sufficient. Too independent. I don't know if you understand what I mean." She paused strategically, drawing breath for the full onslaught. "I really blame myself for this, though."

"Mom, it's really not anyone's—"

"I was the one who told you to go out there and make a career for yourself. I never told you what men were really like. What you had to do to make sure you didn't end up old and alone."

Marcel sighed. Clearly, she was just going to have to suffer through the entire thing in silence.

"You see, darling girl . . . men . . . men really like it when you act helpless and needy. It makes them feel strong, powerful, like real men. It doesn't really matter if you're actually like that or not. The whole point is that you have to make them think that you are. It brings out all of their protective instincts. Do you see what I mean?"

Marcel muttered a barely audible, "Yes."

"Good," her mother said, and her voice brightened considerably. "You see, after you get married, you can decide how you really want to act. Or you can just be yourself. By then, though, it'll be too late for him to figure out exactly what hit him. He'll be caught, you see. And that's what you want. Do you understand?"

Marcel gritted her teeth. "Yes, Mother."

"You have to be aggressive but smart. Let the man do some things for you. Even if you can do them better than he can, you can't let him know that. And cook him a meal at least once a week. I know you modern women have this thing against taking care of your man, but let me tell you, a man is a man is a man. A hundred years ago, today, or a hundred years from now. They all want the same things. And they all like to be taken care of. You have to weave your way into his life. Become indispensable to him."

Marcel made a little noncommittal sound and her mother, listening sharply on the other end of the line, pounced.

"Well, will you try it? Just for a few weeks? Drop this whole career woman thing just for a few weeks? I know you're trying to fix your father's old magazine up, but this is more important. This is your life we're talking about. And if your dad was here now, he'd want you to do the same thing."

Marcel pressed the balls of her palms to her temples. "Sure, Mother," she said. "Why not?" There was no disagreeing with her mother. It was always easier to just go with the flow.

"Good," she said, sounding especially happy now. "Not that you really need to worry yet, honey girl. Most women in our family don't go into menopause until they're at least forty."

Marcel swallowed, and her heart shuddered with dread at her mother's next words: "There was Aunt Sally, though. She started getting hot flashes at about thirty-five. Just five years older than you are right now. But don't let that worry you. There's technology these days. They can do all sorts of things now that they couldn't do fifteen, twenty years ago.

Well . . ." And there was a note of deep satisfaction in her mother's voice now. "I've got to run, sweetheart. But call me tomorrow. OK?"

Marcel hung up and went in search of another tub of ice cream. She opened the freezer door and rooted around for a second, tossing empty boxes into the garbage can behind her. Just her luck. No more ice cream or cheesecake or chocolate fudge bars.

She slammed the door shut again while muttering a string of vile things beneath her breath. *Nothing at all to eat but fruit and yogurt. Now what could she do with that?* If she had some whipped cream and sugar, maybe she might be able to do something interesting. She wrenched the fridge door open again and peered around inside. *Of course.* No whipped cream, and the solitary box of sugar was now a solid block of dark brown caramel.

She slammed the door and stomped off to her bedroom to sulk. No man and no food. What a mess she was in. And now she had another axe hanging over her head. Menopause. And the way things were going, probably before she was thirty-five.

Chapter Twelve

Marcel woke to a supremely quiet Sunday morning full of nothing but wonderful silence and the occasional whistle of wind through the shaggy heads of the half a dozen or so dwarf palms lining the curb just in front of the house. It was the kind of day that she loved. And she was determined that it was going to be better than the day before. She already had it planned. She was going to go grocery shopping first, and then spend the rest of the day lazing about listening to Ella Fitzgerald and Duke Ellington records. She might give Tracy a call at around dinnertime, but only if she absolutely felt like it. With this new-found peace bubbling inside of her, she felt as though anything at all might be possible. She felt strong, powerful, unique.

She walked across to a large window now and

pushed it open. Wonderful breezes swept the room immediately. She leaned both elbows on the sill and rested her chin in her cupped palms. San Diego was truly a beautiful county, and one of these days in the not so distant future she was going to buy a house right on the very lip of the beach. It would have to be a relatively modest one to begin with, but eventually she would be able to afford exactly the kind of house she really wanted. She would have a pool, a Jacuzzi . . . Her eyes took on a dreamy expression. And yes, she would have a wraparound deck with a huge barbecue grill snugly fitted into a corner somewhere. And her husband would barbecue various meats each weekend. Thick steaks dripping with sweet sauce, succulent hamburgers, spicy hot dogs. And they would invite all of their friends to enjoy the hot sunshine, the beach . . . life.

She sucked in a deep breath and let it out slowly. Things were going to work out. There was no need for impatience. Good things were going to come her way. She could feel it. For some inexplicable reason, she felt confident now. And confident women were always poised. They didn't make scenes, not even when they discovered that their man had invited them on a romantic weekend getaway and was also sleeping with the woman in the adjacent cabin. They didn't scream, throw things, cut every piece of his clothing to shreds, and then throw him naked and shivering into the woods. No. Only women who didn't understand that better things were headed their way behaved like that. Such a man, *like her exboyfriend Alex,* was to be politely shown to the door, even if deep down, every single last instinct told you to plant a stiletto heel firmly in the middle of his posterior as the door swung closed behind him. Women who were in control of things did not under any circumstances behave in such an unrestrained manner.

Marcel walked into the bathroom and turned the shower to steaming hot. She was going to have an extra-long bath. She would wash her hair, curl it, and then take herself off to the store.

She shed her clothes quickly and stepped onto the scale and then into the shower cubicle. After her ice-cream-eating binge of the night before, she had succeeded in gaining another two pounds. This might have bothered her to the extreme just twenty-four hours ago, but today, today she didn't care. So what if she had a little flesh on her bones? She was just thick and healthy, and some men liked that.

She poured a silver dollar–sized amount of shampoo into the palm of her hand, turned so that the shower drenched her hair, and then massaged the silky concoction into each strand. She gave her scalp a good rub, wiped some foam from the curl of an ear, and listened. *What was that noise?* The morning had been so peaceful. Now one of the neighbors, because the weather was so gorgeous, had decided to pollute the quiet with a lawn mower.

She finished shampooing her hair, spent a few minutes more conditioning, and then turned off the shower. There was no point to bathing any longer. The noise coming from what sounded very much like just beneath her bedroom window had spoilt everything. She could barely hear herself think now. Why couldn't they have waited until after she had left for the store?

She dried off rapidly, wrapped her head in a thick white towel, and then stepped into her pink-and-white terry cloth robe. She padded on bare feet from the bathroom and winced as the racket hit her full blast.

She hurried across the room to close the window, and stopped dead. There was someone standing in the middle of her little overgrown patch of lawn. A man in a superbly fitted pair of jeans, a white T-shirt with rolled sleeves, and long well-muscled brown arms. Her heart began a slow and heavy pounding in her chest. It couldn't be.

And, almost as though he had been aware of her regard, he turned and looked directly up at the window. Marcel closed her eyes for an instant. *What was he doing here?* Was he completely out of his mind?

She opened up the window again and leaned out. "What're you doing?" she bellowed above the noise of the motor.

He cut the engine and wiped a hand across his brow. "I told you last night that your grass needed cutting. It's not good to let it get this long."

Marcel pulled in her bottom lip and then let it back out with a little plop. This was a very confusing situation. Most men she rejected were gone an instant after her lack of interest was made clear to them. So why was Ian Michaels haunting her every footstep? She couldn't understand it all. He should be able to tell just by looking at her house that she didn't have a lot of money. So if he was some sort of gigolo, why was he still here? He couldn't be hard up for sex, either. A man with his kind of looks would have to beat women off with a broom. So, what was it? It wasn't that he wanted to be her friend, either. And she didn't believe for a second that he really found her attractive in an irresistible kind of way.

"I'll be finished with the entire thing in about half an hour, so don't let me disturb whatever you were doing."

Marcel's hand went directly to the towel wrapped about her head. Lord. She had forgotten that it was there. She popped back behind the billowing curtain and then went across to sit on the bed. Her fingers were cold. Her feet were cold. But the rest of her was burning hot. Hot and wet. Seeing him in those tight jeans with that firm, hard behind and those long, long arms. God. It was almost too much for her to take. It had been such a long time since she had lain with a man in that manner, and she had needs. She was a grown woman after all, and a very healthy one.

She pressed a balled fist to the hot point between her thighs, closed her eyes, and tried to breathe her way out of her current distress. And as she did, she counted and muttered beneath her breath, "One. Two. Three. Come on, you can do it. He's just a man. Just a man. A pretty package. A pretty, empty package. Just flesh and bones. He's nothing special."

She swallowed on a dry throat and allowed an errant thought to sneak into the back of her mind. Yes, she was looking for a serious relationship, someone completely unlike the men of her past. But did that mean that, in the meantime, she couldn't have a completely meaningless affair? What if she did? What would happen? Would the sky fall? Would the ground open up and swallow her whole? She propped her chin on the ball of a palm.

She opened her eyes and removed her fist. No. She wouldn't do it. She'd be strong. She'd focus on her plan. On her rules. That's what she'd do.

Marcel got up and headed for the bathroom. She was going to have to take another shower. A cold one this time. And if Ian Michaels was going to keep popping up in this unexpected manner wearing his tight jeans and even tighter T-shirts, she was going to have to get accustomed to having a lot of cold showers.

Chapter Thirteen

It was almost an hour before Marcel was through with her hair. She spent an extra-long time blowing it dry and then another stretch curling it into meticulously done corkscrew tendrils. The noise from the lawn mower had stopped more than half an hour ago, and she prayed that Ian had gotten into his truck and left. But she had a sneaking suspicion that he was still lurking around somewhere.

She went back to the window and peered out in a cautious manner. Where in the name of heaven was he? His truck was still parked on the gravel drive, so he was still here. Well, she would have to go and find him to thank him for his work on the lawn. The grass was now a neat half an inch high. She had to admit that the little yard looked completely different now. He had done a very good job. Marcel stepped away from the window and walked rapidly through the tiny sitting room and into the kitchen. She began opening and closing drawers and removing various utensils. She should fix him something to eat. Offering him money seemed kind of tacky, so offering him food was the least she could do. Just a few sandwiches. Some ice-cold lemonade. It wouldn't take her a minute. She would invite him in for just a moment, let him eat, and then send him on his way.

She moved about the kitchen quickly and efficiently. Bread from the bread bin. Good yellow butter. Cheese. Cold slices of ham and roast beef. Iceberg lettuce still crunchy at the edges. A dash of spicy mustard. Circles of onion. And a sprinkle of black pepper.

She sliced the edges off each piece of bread and then cut the stack of sandwiches into triangles.

The lemonade was done with equal speed. Two large yellow lemons juiced by hand. The pulp and seeds strained. Water and golden syrup added. Then thick chunks of ice accompanied by much stirring.

When Marcel was satisfied with the taste, she found a large glass jug with pretty sunflowers on its pouting belly and filled it almost to the brim with the ice-cold beverage. She removed some paper napkins from one of the drawers.

She padded to the front door in her bedroom slippers. She had resisted the urge to put on heels. It had been a ridiculous impulse. It would have suggested to anyone with an eye to see that she had some sort of an interest in the man she was about to invite into her house. That she actually cared about how she might appear to him. But she didn't care. Not at all.

She opened the door and stood for a moment on the threshold, enjoying the beautiful mid-morning breeze. It was not yet as hot as it was going to get, but the sun was already high in the sky and the day had taken on an unusual blue-gold quality. She hesitated for just a moment more and then took the narrow stone path around to the side of the house. She rounded the corner and came to an abrupt halt. He was standing in the middle of the yard with his back to her. Shirtless.

Her eyes ran the length of his back and she absorbed with some amount of bemusement that there was not a single ripple of fat anywhere in sight. His shoulders were broad and muscular. And there was the most intriguing furrow running the entire length of his back. It was the kind of indentation that lent itself perfectly to the stroke of a finger or tongue. . . .

Since it was apparent that he was completely unaware of her presence, she cleared her throat, and croaked something that was barely intelligible even to her own ears.

He turned, and the view of his chest with its sleekly formed six-pack of muscles made her rush hastily into speech again.

"I'm hot . . . I mean it's . . . it's hot and lemonade and sandwiches inside." Hot embarrassed blood rushed to her throat and cheeks. What in the name of heaven was the matter with her? She was stuttering like a teenager with her first major crush. This never happened to her. Not with any man. And she had run across some *very* good-looking ones in her time.

He seemed to understand her broken offer, though, because he approached with what could only be described as a deeply pleased smile on his face.

"You made food for me?"

Marcel gestured with a hand. "It was the least I could do. And it's getting kind of warm anyway and I'm sure you must be hungry after all that mowing." She tried her level best not to stare at his wonderful chest. Instead, she focused deliberately on his amber eyes. No relief there. She noted with some amount of confusion that his eyes appeared kind. Generous, even.

"So, do I get to come inside, or will you throw me the food from the kitchen window?"

Marcel chuckled before she could prevent herself. "Don't be silly. Of course you're invited inside."

She turned and sashayed back to the front door, all the while keenly aware that she was perhaps swinging her hips from side to side just a little more than was completely natural. She felt his eyes on her the entire way and she wondered in a slightly distracted manner if the two pounds she had put on overnight showed on her hips.

He was just half a pace behind her now, and Marcel tried not to hurry. She didn't want him to sense what kind of an effect he was having on her.

"Have a seat," she said once they were inside. Her voice was cool, calm, but her heart was beating in a strangely lopsided manner in her chest.

"You have a nice home," he said when he was comfortably seated on the long sofa. And before Marcel could even think of an appropriate response to that, he was asking her something else entirely. And his question, although politely put, caused her to say in a very bald manner, "What?"

He scratched the back of an ear with a finger and said again, "I asked if you had run into anyone else interesting. I know you're not going to see that guy from last night again."

Marcel lifted the jug of lemonade from where it sat on the counter, placed it on a large tray, and then busied herself with the sandwiches. He was truly an extremely rude man. How could he just come out and ask her a question like that? Were they close friends? Had she given him any sign at all that she would be open to having this kind of discussion with him?

"It's nothing to be ashamed of," he said now, interrupting her train of thought. "Since we've agreed to be friends, maybe I can help point you away from some of the more unsavory characters." Then he laughed in a manner that caused a skitter of heat to warm her from head to toe. "I didn't get to be this old without picking up a thing or two. Besides, I'm a man, so I understand how men think. I know the code."

"You're just incredible," Marcel said, picking up the tray. "Why are you so interested in helping me? I've been trying to figure it out, and nothing's making any sense to me."

He looked at her for a long moment, and in that stretch of silence Marcel crossed to the coffee table and set the tray before him.

"So?" she continued without preamble. "What exactly do you want?" If he could be blunt, then so could she.

He picked up one of the paper plates on the tray, handed it to her, and then selected another for himself.

"Do I have to want something? Sit." He gestured as she continued to stand over him. "I'm completely harmless. I promise you."

Marcel considered ignoring his suggestion but after a moment decided that to do so would be silly. So she perched herself gingerly on the opposite end of the sofa and allowed puzzlement to pool in the depths of her eyes. There was something about him that she had never noticed before. Perhaps because she had not spent any particular time with him before now. Last evening didn't count, of course. She'd been half-blind then and in general distress over how haywire the evening had gone. But now, now she noticed it. There was an air of authority about him, of confidence.

"I don't want anything from you that you don't want to give me," he said.

She turned toward him, speculation alight in her dark eyes. She just couldn't seem to figure him out. It was all very puzzling.

"Well," she said now, "I won't be giving you anything at all. So, if you have some sort of devious plan in the back of your mind, you can just forget all about it. I know your unusual interest in me has nothing to do with the fact that you find me irresistibly attractive."

He bit into his sandwich and chewed. "Has no one ever found you irresistible? A woman who looks as you do? I find that hard to believe."

Marcel calmly reached for a sandwich. He was beginning to wreak havoc on her nerves. She had decided to completely ignore his question. There was no point to answering it, as far as she could see. Besides, she was far too old for that sort of nonsense anyway. She was thirty years old, for goodness' sake. A grown woman by anyone's standards.

Instead she sipped from her glass and then said in a pleased manner, "Wouldn't you like some of this lemonade? It's very good. Not too sweet."

He smiled, aware that she was ignoring him. "No, thank you. You were about to tell me about these other men you're dating."

Marcel laughed despite herself. "I was about to do nothing of the sort." And she prepared to rise.

But he reached across and, before she could prevent it, captured one of her arms. "Don't go," he said. And his thumb stroked gently across her skin.

Marcel's eyes widened, but she remained where she was.

"Look at me."

Again, that strange authority in his voice. Marcel shifted her gaze from the food tray to his golden amber eyes. And what she saw there caused a blend of fear and excitement to pound its way through her blood.

"What do you want from me?" she whispered.

His fingers slid down her arm to unclench her fingers. Then his thumb dipped to caress the soft center of her palm.

"I want . . . you," he said.

Chapter Fourteen

Marcel sat stock-still, her mind churning. It had been a mistake. A huge error in judgment. She should never have invited him into the house. He had quite obviously misunderstood her intentions.

She dragged her hand free and got to her feet, her eyes sparkling with the remnants of conflicted desire.

"I thought you had this in mind when you showed up here today. Well, let me tell you something."

"Yes, tell me." And he sat back and regarded her with the steady eyes of a jungle cat that was on the verge of devouring its prey.

"I've had men like you before. Exactly like you. And I'm never going there again. Never."

"You mean you would never consider someone like me for a long-term relationship?"

"Exactly." Marcel nodded. "That's exactly what I mean."

"OK. Fair enough. We could have a short-term relationship, though, right? An affair? I could be your maintenance man. Do all of those little things you like." And his eyes ran slowly from the peaks of her breasts, down her legs, and then back up again.

Marcel's mouth opened in a little plop of sound. *No, he didn't just say that to her.*

"Are you completely out of your mind?"

He leaned back in the chair and crossed one leg over the other in a manner that drew Marcel's attention to the long, muscular length of him. He had the appearance of a powerful man in every sense of the word.

"We're both adults. We can talk to each other frankly, can't we?"

Marcel pressed her lips together. She really and truly did not know what to make of him. He was so, so . . .

"I don't have a problem with speaking frankly. In fact, I prefer it myself."

"Good." He smiled. "I know I sprang this on you. But will you promise to at least think about it?" And he got to his feet, making the room appear suddenly small and crowded. "If the idea appeals to you, make a list of everything you'd like me to do while we're together, OK? And I do mean everything. Nothing is off-limits."

Then he left her standing there in the middle of the living room floor, numb, confused . . . and thoughtful.

Chapter Fifteen

Monday, despite the cheerful weather of the previous day, was gray and overcast, and Marcel found herself in almost as dark a mood as she sat at her desk. She had spent the better part of the morning wrestling with a mixture of problems, each one more serious than the last. First, she had had a bellowing match with the printer over a four-color proof that had not been colorized to her satisfaction. Then, following quickly on the heels of that, the celebrity who'd been booked for the next issue's cover suddenly and without explanation decided to back out of the photo shoot.

Marcel lifted a hand to massage the tense muscles at the base of her neck. She had awoken with a sore neck, and now with the mounting stress, it was clear that by the end of the day the soreness would have worked its way down the stretch of her back.

She turned toward the window and glared at the gathering storm clouds. There was no doubt at all in her mind as to what was behind this sudden spate of calamities. She had turned down Tyson Media's offer to buy her out just weeks before in a terse little letter that could have left them in no doubt as to her feelings on the matter. She'd received a personal call from the vice president of Tyson very soon after, much to her surprise, and had been forced to spend another half an hour reconfirming what she had said so clearly in the letter. She had turned down his offer of dinner and had assured him that there was absolutely nothing he could do to change her mind. He had laughed heartily at that and had told her very nicely that everything was simply a matter of negotiation. And that she would sell her magazine to them sooner or later. But sell she most certainly would.

Marcel had hung up at that point and then directed a few choice words at the Monet prints hanging on her office walls. She would never sell. Never. She had made her father this promise as he lay on his sickbed five years before. And she intended to keep it. No strong-arm tactics would succeed in making her give in, either. She wasn't beaten. Not by a long shot. She hadn't even begun to fight yet. *La Beau Monde* would remain in the family. Her father had given the publication his life's blood. It had probably even been the reason that his marriage had broken up. He had worked on it night and day, week in and week out. And finally, five years ago, the little magazine that could had, through very hard work, managed to become the premiere magazine on the West Coast for the urban professional. But its new stature had been a mixed blessing. Large media conglomerates began tracking their progress. Then the buyout offers began. And, in the middle of it all, her father became sick. Many years of heavy smoking, combined with a serious case of cirrhosis of the liver. He had lingered for a few weeks, his body gone frail and dry. His eyes rheumy and suddenly showing their age. Marcel had sat at his bedside and listened with damp eyes to all of his frantic instructions. He had tried to give her a lifetime's worth of knowledge in just days. He had warned her about Tyson. They were the most dangerous of the entire lot, he had told her. If they couldn't have the magazine, they would destroy it. They were one of the most aggressive business entities around. Their policy was to take no prisoners. You were either with them or out of business. Well, two could play this game.

Marcel turned toward her desk now and reached for the phone.

"Jules," she said as soon as her assistant picked up. "I want you to set up a lunch meeting with the Tyson team. Let them know that I've changed my mind about the acquisition, and that I'd like to meet to discuss terms."

She was greeted by stunned silence, and then her assistant, who had seen the publication through many of the lean years, asked in a pinched voice, "You're going to sell?"

Marcel tapped the back of her pen on the smooth face of the desk. "I'm not going to sell, but I'm definitely going to play their game, Jules. We can't hope to win this fight if we play it straight down the middle. Don't worry, though," and her voice softened. "Everything'll be fine. Trust me. OK? Set up the meeting for . . ." and she leaned forward to check the flat desk calendar, "three weeks from today. Either the Monday or Friday of that week. Also see if you can find out for me who owns Tyson. And, Jules," she said in response to what sounded suspiciously like a sniffle, "we're not going to lose the magazine. No matter what happens. So, don't start crying yet."

She replaced the receiver in its cradle and sat for a moment staring into space. It would have been nice to have a man in her life, one she could bounce ideas off of. She would have plotted strategy with him. It was too bad, just too bad, that she hadn't found him yet. She understood fully about waiting and being patient. But she felt so all alone sometimes. She was strong and independent, but every superwoman needed a day off from time to time.

A frown rippled her forehead. Would a pretty boy like Ian Michaels be completely at sea in this kind of cutthroat environment? Sure he knew a thing or two about romancing women. He could quite probably write an entire book on the subject. But would he be any help to her at all in the business environment? Her eyes became thoughtful. Players were notoriously skilled at strategy, though. Players with smooth, hard bodies, firm, thick thighs, and cute little buttocks.

Marcel unlocked her middle drawer and removed a delicate white fan. Lord, would she like to see him in a little black G-string. Muscles rippling, skin just begging for the gentle stroke of her tongue.

She fanned herself vigorously and her eyes sparkled with sudden thought. Since her date on Saturday she'd been thinking about it, and she was completely convinced that this little alteration in her rules would make all the difference in the world. She wouldn't go on another agency date until she resolved this issue with Tyson Media, but when she did, she wanted to make sure that she had every possible chance of success.

She folded the little fan closed and replaced it in her desk drawer. Four weeks at least until the problem with Tyson was resolved. And at least another week before she actually went out on another date. And only God alone knew how long until she would again find a man to share her bed. She sighed and ran a hand across the sore muscles in her neck. Ian Michael's proposition was beginning to look more and more tempting now that she'd had more time to think about it carefully. Why couldn't she, an adult woman of the grand old age of thirty, take a lover if she so desired? Especially if they both understood the nature of the relationship. No strings. No expectations of marriage. No pressure to spend every single last waking moment together. Hot, totally uninhibited, soul-satisfying sex. With the appropriate precautions taken, of course.

She put the pen down because her grip had grown damp. She needed this. She was going into her sexual peak years. So, why couldn't she? She understood her rules. She now knew how to protect her heart. How to prevent it from being broken yet again.

Her eyes took on a bright glitter. The more she thought about the entire thing, the more sense it seemed to make. Why deny herself until she found the right man? Men didn't.

She looked up guiltily when someone knocked softly on her door.

"Come in!" she called out.

"These just came for you," the receptionist said with an as-pleased-as-punch expression on her face. And she came forward with a large bouquet of pure white roses.

Marcel's heart gave a hard thump in her chest,

and she did her best to stand firmly on the hazy feeling of happiness that rose sharply in her eyes.

"Just put them on the desk please, Rhonda." She gestured in what she hoped was a suitably offhanded manner.

"A secret admirer?" the girl asked with mischievous eyes.

Marcel merely gave her a tolerant smile. "What does the card say?"

Rhonda whipped the nicely embossed white card from its envelope. "It says," and she squinted at the elegant print, " 'A cup of warm soup. A pair of warm arms. A fireplace overlooking the sea. Life's little treasures can lead to life's little pleasures. Let me know as soon as you decide.' " She turned the card over and back. "No name, though."

A little smile flickered about Marcel's lips. He was so arrogant. He felt sure that he was the only one sending her flowers.

"You know who they're from?" Rhonda still lingered, anxious to know who had sent such an elegant offering.

Marcel nodded. "I know who they're from. And don't ask me who," she said, a mock note of severity in her voice.

Rhonda gave her a bubbly smile. Everyone in the office knew that Marcel was a generous and kindhearted boss who hardly ever had a harsh word to say to any of her employees.

"OK," the girl said, not put out at all. "I guess I'd better just go on back to my phones."

When she had gone, Marcel walked around to the front of her desk to inspect the flowers. It was a special basket arrangement, unusually done with each green stem supported by a bed of foam. She ran a gentle finger across a petal. The roses were vibrant soft-headed beauties with delicate creamy hearts, furled lips, and the most divine fragrance.

She pulled one of the long stems from within and buried her nose deep in its center. It had been such a long time since any man had even thought to send her roses. And Ian Michaels was the devil himself, because this was exactly the button to press with her right now. She needed romance, affection, touching, caring . . .

She picked up the phone again after a long moment of reflection. Dialed.

"Tracy," she said when the phone was answered. "What're you doing tonight? I've got to talk to you about something."

Chapter Sixteen

A few hours later, Ian drove the coast road, his truck pointed in the direction of the small San Diego airport. He was picking up Daniella today. He had sent her to spend the weekend in New York with her mother, although he had had serious misgivings about doing so. Whenever the child returned from one of these little visits, she always reverted to screaming tantrums and nights of bed-wetting. So he was very worried about what might be awaiting him on this occasion.

He turned into airport parking, found a spot after only short minutes of searching, and was soon walking briskly toward the small arrivals area. He allowed his thoughts to drift for a moment to Marcel. She would have gotten his roses by now. Women loved flowers, so they were bound to make her

soften in her attitude toward him. But if they didn't
do the trick, he had additional surprises in store for
her. Whatever it took to get her he was willing to
do. He was determined to have her. And it would be
worth it when he did. He saw the pent-up passion in
her. The need. The fire. She would be a tigress in
bed. He saw that, too. And, at this point in his life,
after many years of controlled self-denial, such a
woman was exactly what he needed. And the entire
arrangement would be perfect, because it would be
a completely no-strings-attached affair.

"Mr. Michaels," said a severely harassed-
sounding voice.

Ian turned. "Where is she?" he asked his personal
assistant.

Bob Wilson, a tall man of over six feet with the
bulk and poundage to intimidate the most worthy of
assailants, gave Ian the kind of look that smacked of
fear. "She's still on the plane," he said.

Ian's brows lifted. "On the plane?" He checked
his watch just to be absolutely certain. "They arrived
more than half an hour ago."

His personal assistant nodded. "Yes, well . . .
there's a little problem."

"Problem? What kind of problem? Is she sick?"

"No, no, nothing like that," Bob rushed to assure
him. "It's just that she's refusing to leave the plane."

Ian's chest moved in silent laughter. "Refusing?

You mean no one on board can handle a child of seven?"

His personal assistant followed him as Ian strode rapidly toward the arrival gate.

"There's something else."

"What else?" Ian asked without breaking his stride.

Bob's voice cracked a bit, and Ian shot him a lightning glance. He had never seen the man this unnerved before, and they had both been involved in many a situation over the years.

"She's, ah . . . tied herself to something or other in the rest room and I think she's done some damage to the lavatory area."

Ian stopped. "What?"

Bob wiped a trickle of perspiration from the side of a temple. "I managed to convince them to wait until you got here. But things are serious. They were thinking of calling the authorities because no one can get within six feet of her."

"Well, we'll soon see about that." And Ian strode rapidly toward the mouth of the gate. He was immediately greeted by an airline official who had the look of a man who had just suffered through the most trying of ordeals.

"Mr. Michaels?" the man asked, a faint note of hope in his voice. "I'm so glad you're here. She was fine on the flight over. Behaved as good as gold, she did. But something seemed . . . I don't know what happened, but as soon as we arrived at the gate—"

"It's OK," Ian assured the worried man. "She just recently lost her father and she's . . ." He clapped the man on the shoulder. "I'll get her out. Don't worry."

Earsplitting shrieks greeted Ian as soon as he stepped onto the plane. And his eyes went immediately to the small crowd of people huddled just before the forward lavatory door in the first-class cabin. The group turned as one at his approach.

"She seems to be having an episode," a tall flight attendant with a long and humorless face remarked. "It might be a good idea to call a doctor."

Ian gave the woman a cold look. "I'm her uncle. And no doctor will be called. Step aside please," he said to the small crowd.

He pushed the lavatory door, took a deep breath, and said in a gravelly voice, "Daniella, stop that screaming right now."

The little girl gave him a baleful stare, opened her mouth, and bellowed even harder. Ian stepped into the tiny bathroom and closed the door behind him.

"Now," he said. "It's just you and me. What're you crying and carrying on like this about? Don't you want to come back and live with your poor lonely uncle? You told me that you liked living by the ocean, remember? And now, Vera and I have got your bedroom all fixed up for you. Just the way I know you'll like it. You can see the waves breaking on the sand from your bedroom window. And maybe even a dolphin or two."

He continued to speak in a light and soothing manner, reminding her of the house, the beach, the sand, the tiny pink crabs. And, after a minute of this, the little girl gave a large hiccup, rubbed a grubby fist across an eye, and said, "But I don't want to go to heaven yet."

With some difficulty because of the cramped space, Ian managed to lower himself to her level.

"What do you mean, honey?"

"Mommy . . . Mommy said," she confided through many burbling hiccups, "that if I was good I would go to heaven one day soon. Then I'd be able to see my daddy."

Ian pressed a hand to his mouth. Why had her mother told her that? Didn't the woman understand how frightening a concept that would be to a little child? He really should have followed his mind and not sent Daniella back to New York on her own.

"Your mommy meant that one day a very, very long time from now you, me, and everyone we love will go to heaven. But you don't have to worry about it, honey. You're going to be with me for a long, long time," he assured her in a gentle voice.

She looked at Ian with large distrustful eyes. "But Daddy didn't stay with us for a long time. He left me all alone . . . and he went away without even telling me he was going."

"No, you're right," Ian agreed. "But the same thing won't happen to you, OK? Or me. Because I am your daddy's big brother. And big brothers always stick around to take care of things. So that means I'll be here for a good long while. And I can be your second daddy . . . if you want me to?"

The little head shook. "I want my real daddy, not a pretend one."

"OK," Ian consoled. "Tell you what. If you let me untie you, we'll talk it over some more in my truck. Daddy's truck. Does that sound like a plan?"

She gave him a watery, "Yes."

Ian continued talking. "And maybe, if you like, we'll stop and get some ice cream on the way home. Would you like that?"

Again a nod and a sodden affirmative.

Ian smiled. "OK then. So, let's not have any more of this crying then. Uncle is here, and Uncle will always be here. I promise you that. Now," and he stroked a long tear from the flat of her face, "take your foot out of the toilet bowl."

Chapter Seventeen

Marcel slid into the hard leather booth and waved a hand in the air.

"Tracy . . . over here. Over here." The little jazz bar in La Jolla was one of the trendiest spots on the West Coast. It was well known for its good food and even better jazz. It was always crowded, even on rainy Monday nights. But Marcel had chosen to make a reservation there because she had made an important decision.

"Tracy!" she called, this time standing up so that her friend might better see her through the teeming mass of bodies.

Tracy caught sight of her and waved in return. Marcel waited until her friend had managed to make it to the booth before sitting again.

"God," Tracy said as soon as she slid into the

booth. "Can you believe this place? Excuse me," and she turned in her seat to address a man who had just placed his very sizable rear end on the lip of the booth.

The man turned, mug of beer in hand. "Well now," he said. "You ladies need some company?" And he leaned forward to confide in an alcoholic gush, "What you need, baby, is a real man. I'm taking care of two women like you right now. You know what I'm saying? Cars. Apartments. The whole nine. Think you can handle it?"

Tracy opened her pocketbook with a fluid movement of her hand. "I've got some pepper spray in here. Think you can handle that?"

The man gave her a bleary-eyed look. "I'm hearing you," he said, and he melted back into the crowd without further comment.

Marcel chuckled heartily. "Aw, come on now, Tracy, you know that was just cruel. He just wanted to take care of you. Make you one of his women. Buy you a car. Get you an apartment. Why would you turn down an offer like that?"

Tracy rolled her eyes. "Please. He needs to take care of himself first before he can even think about taking care of anybody else. Did you see the amount of gold in his mouth?"

Marcel shook her head and said with a note of wicked fun in her voice, "The opportunities you let pass you by. And you tell me that I'm slow on the uptake when it comes to men."

Tracy gave her a speaking look and Marcel chuckled again.

"Anyway," she said, and leaned forward to declare excitedly, "you'll never guess what happened?"

Tracy zipped her bag closed. "Don't tell me you've decided to give Bill crazy butt Cook another chance? Girl, you have to know when to let go. There are plenty of other men out there, you know? I don't want to start on Ian Michaels again, but you should really—"

"No, no," Marcel stopped her. "Of course it's not *Bill Cook*. Do you think I'm crazy, too?"

Tracy gave her a noncommittal look. "Well, I don't know. Of late—"

Marcel clicked her tongue. "Just shut up and listen." And she spread her fingers on the table. "I've thought about this good and long and I've made up my mind about it." She took a breath and then said in a very steady and reasonable manner, "I'm going to have an affair."

Tracy put her glass of water back on the table with a thump and regarded Marcel with surprised eyes.

"An affair? With . . . with whom? Marcy honey, you haven't just gone out and picked up some—"

"Girl, please," Marcel interrupted. "What do you think I am? I'm talking about Ian Michaels."

Tracy reached across to grab her hand. "Ian Michaels? Oh, my God, you've finally come to your senses. What brought this on? Did he come back after I left on Saturday night? Come on, come on, tell me."

Marcel held on to the smile playing around the corners of her mouth. "If you'd only shut up for a minute, I'd be able to tell you what I'm talking about."

"OK." Tracy nodded, and she made a little locking motion with one of her hands. "I'm not going to say anything else." She folded her hands before her on the tabletop. "So, tell me."

"Well," and Marcel leaned forward with sparkling eyes. "I'd been thinking about everything, you know? About what you said and about the fact that for whatever reason, he seems to be interested in me." She paused to take a sip of water. "I mean, he's not the right man for me obviously, according to my rules, according to our rules. But that doesn't mean we can't have a short-term thing, right? While I keep looking?"

Tracy gave a deep chuckle and asked, "Wait a second, is this really you talking? Miss prim and proper? Miss 'I've got to do everything exactly by the book'?"

"I know, I know," Marcel said, and she reached forward to select a chip from the bowl that sat between them, dipped a healthy portion of salsa, placed it in her mouth, and crunched. "But," she said after a bit, "I've been without a man for a while, haven't I?"

Tracy took a chip and agreed heartily, "You have, girl. You have. And I don't know how you do it, either. I mean, the longest I've ever gone is. . . ." she paused for an instant to think about it, ". . . maybe a week. But you can go for years." She laughed. "I could *never* do that. I've got to get my good and plenty every night. You know what I'm talking about?"

Marcel nodded. "Well, I'm going to get mine now. Ian Michaels is a fine-looking man. I mean, I know he's not interested in anything serious, but that's OK. Since I know all that going in, my expectations will be different. And it'll be worth it, too, because body-wise . . . he is stacked. And not just in the back, either."

Tracy chortled. "So you noticed the hands and the fingers, huh?"

Marcel leaned forward. "I noticed everything. Yesterday, he came by and— You know that patch of long grass outside? You can't even really call it a lawn. Well, he cut the whole thing. Looks really good now, too. And he took his shirt off, and girl," she fanned herself with a hand, "I almost had to go take a third shower."

Tracy's eyebrows lifted. "Third?"

"Oh, I was already on my second by the time he

started on the grass. He had on this T-shirt and these jeans. I've never seen clothes fit a man's body like that before."

Tracy tapped a nail on the table. "But how're you going to put it to him, though? You don't want to make it seem . . ." she wiggled the fingers on one hand, ". . . you know."

Marcel motioned for a waiter and almost instantly a man in a brightly colored tunic peeled away from the crowd and came to stand by the table.

"Yes, ladies. What can I get for you?"

"More nachos please," Marcel said with a warm little smile. "And a mudslide for me and . . ." She looked at Tracy.

Tracy gave Marcel an impatient look and said, "A strawberry daiquiri."

The man melted back into the crowd, and Tracy said, "So, stop stalling. How're you going to approach him? That's really important, you know. There's an art to how you do it. If you say the wrong thing to him, he'll just treat you like a good-time thing. Nothing serious."

"Haven't you been listening to anything I've been saying?" Marcel asked. And there was a trace of impatience in her voice now. "This entire thing with Ian Michaels isn't going to be serious. And he understands that. He actually said that he'd be my maintenance man . . . if I was interested."

Tracy pushed her glass aside. "What? And you let him get away with that?"

Marcel shrugged. "I don't care. Why can't you understand what I'm telling you? He's the wrong type. Can you really imagine me having a long-term relationship with a man like that? After he got tired of me he'd probably start messing around with every woman under eighty. He'd probably run me into bankruptcy, too . . . lose me the magazine." She made a little sound of disgust. "He'll just be fulfilling a biological need. Nothing more. Nothing less. And when I talk to him about it, I'm going to tell him that, too. Just so he doesn't get the wrong impression and come away thinking that I have any sort of long-term interest in him. He said he believes in people being direct. So, that's how I'm going to put it to him. Directly."

Tracy's mouth was tight by the time Marcel had concluded her little speech. "You know," she said, "I never thought I'd say this about you, but it's completely clear to me now. You're just plain old-fashioned stupid, aren't you? Yes," she said as Marcel drew breath to interrupt. "You are a very stupid woman. Put your rules aside for the moment. Can't you recognize quality when you see it? Ian Michaels is a quality man. And you know how hard it is to find one of those these days. And where do you get off talking about him like that? Do you really know anything about the man's background? He might turn out to be the best thing that's ever happened to you."

Marcel's chin tilted up and her eyes took on a dangerous sparkle. She leaned back in the leather booth and folded both arms across her chest.

"Well, thank you very much for letting me know exactly how you really feel, Mrs. Tracy 'high and mighty, I'm so intelligent and together' Roberts. I'm going to let you in on a little secret now just so there's no confusion later on down the line."

Tracy leaned forward, her eyes beginning to glitter, too. "What secret?"

Marcel waited for the drinks and chips to be placed before them. "I am not inviting you to my wedding when it happens. I want you to know that now."

Tracy's brows lifted. "And how are you going to keep me away?"

Marcel took a taste of the thick chocolate-and-cream drink. "I'll think of something, don't you worry yourself over that. And you can of course forget about being my matron of honor, too. Anyone who'll call me stupid to my face . . . Well, I don't have to say any more than that."

Tracy laughed in a dry manner. "Not only am I going to be at your wedding, but I'm going to be the one in charge of organizing the entire thing. So just cut the drama because I really don't want to hear it right now."

"I'm going to call him tonight," Marcel said after a stretch of silence.

"OK, fine," Tracy said, leaning forward to grip Marcel's hand. "So you're going to tell him . . . how?"

"I'm just going to come out and say it. I'll tell him that I've been thinking his offer over and—"

"Wait a second. Wait a second. You didn't tell me about an offer. You just said—"

"Well, it wasn't anything like what you're thinking," Marcel interrupted. "He just said that . . . that he wanted me. That's all. He was very smooth about it, though. Which told me right away that he's probably used to making these kinds of proposals to all kinds of women. All the time."

"Or maybe you're just special," Tracy said, and she took a long drink from her daiquiri. "Maybe you just do it for him. You can be nice . . . when you put your mind to it."

Marcel tried her best not to smile. "Just shut up," she said. Then, "You know I wasn't serious about what I said just now . . . about you not being my matron of honor if I ever get married?"

Tracy reached out to hold her hand. "Do you think, after all this time, that I pay any attention to you? I know you're crazy."

Marcel laughed. "I might be crazy, but by this time next week, I'm gonna have a warm-blooded man in my bed."

Chapter Eighteen

Ian pulled the blanket up around the sleeping child. It had taken quite a bit of doing to get her to bed. She had calmed down considerably after leaving the airport. He had managed to convince her to let him untie her and then he had carried her piggyback-style out to his truck. An hour or two of shopping for toys, a quick stop for extra large ice-cream cones with sprinkles, and then a long walk along the beach had calmed her to a great degree. But as darkness approached, so had her fears. Ian had held her in his arms and rocked her, promising over and over again that she wouldn't be spirited away in the middle of the night by unseen forces. That he would be right there when she woke up in the morning and that, if she desired it, he would not even leave her side during the night.

She had finally settled into full-blown sleep at just before nine o'clock, lying against his chest with her thumb shoved deep inside her mouth.

Ian got up slowly from the bed now and stood for several pensive minutes, watching Dani as she slept. She was going to require a lot of his time, that much was certain. Maybe once she had gotten over her immediate fear of dying, she'd be easier to handle. His brows wrinkled in thought. What she really needed, of course, was a mother. Someone like Marcel Templeton maybe? He wasn't sure. Only time alone would tell. But until he did find the appropriate woman to marry, he would have to do his best to be both mother and father to Dani. There was no real point in trying to involve her biological mother in her upbringing. The woman, as far as he was concerned, was not a fit parent. She popped in and out of the child's life when it suited her. Whenever she was sober enough to do so, she put in an appearance. But, over the past several years, the visits had become less and less frequent. And now, she hardly bothered at all. She missed birthdays and Christmas with equal regularity, too.

He walked out to the veranda, sat in one of the low deck chairs, removed a pair of spectacles from a smooth leather case on the table, and then reached for the black briefcase at his side. Every night, without fail, he spent several hours going over the business activities of the different divisions of his company, making notes, recording his queries and suggestions on a microcassette recorder. And he did this now, only looking up once to thank his housekeeper for the nightly cup of coffee and sandwiches that she never failed to bring him.

Her parting comment of, "Make sure you don't work too late," was met with a warm smile and a promise that he would not. Then Ian bent to his work again, and did not look up again until the chill in the ocean air began to seep into the thick muscles in his neck.

He moved his head from side to side for a bit, glanced at his watch, and then reached forward to turn the tape recorder off. It was almost midnight, and he had done a satisfactory evening of work. In the morning, he would authorize his CEO to go ahead with the planned acquisition of a number of small magazines in the area. The collective purchase would require a substantial outlay of capital, but it would help cement the company's hold on the West Coast. So, it would be well worth it.

He stood, arched his back in a long feline stretch, and then walked the short distance to the veranda rails. His gaze followed a couple as they walked hand in hand on the beach, and as his eyes followed their progress down the sugary sand, he sighed in a tight manner. It was such a long time since he had indulged in the simple luxury of holding hands with a woman he liked. He had let too many years go by

in the pursuit of a goal he had once seen as being
all-important. But, over the past two years, he had
come to realize that the truly important things were
not the ones he had always thought to be so. Family
was important. Making time for life was important.
Finding a special woman was important. Love was
important. And his relationship with the Almighty,
something he had neglected for quite a while. That
was all-important.

A gust of wind rattled his papers, and he turned
to stack and secure them in a manila folder. He was
going to make some serious changes in his life,
though. No more time would be allowed to simply
slip through his fingers. And maybe Marcel Templeton was just the woman to begin this softer, gentler
part of his life with. . . .

Chapter Nineteen

Marcel passed the remainder of the week in a flurry
of activity. By the end of the day on Thursday, she
had waded through an endless slew of meetings with
her staff, confirmed the Tyson meeting for the first
Friday of the next month, and then scheduled several
lunch appointments with various advertising agency
executives.

Friday afternoon found her seated at her desk going over the copy for the next issue. She reviewed
each line of text in a meticulous and highly focused
manner, penciling in comments here and there, and
pausing every so often to highlight a snatch of words
with a brilliant green highlighter pen. At a few
minutes before four o'clock, she stacked the copy
boards together and then called for her assistant.

"Jules, would you see that these changes are made before you leave?"

Julie Carter appeared in the office doorway almost immediately and Marcel gave her a warm smile.

"Shouldn't take more than an hour or so. I've marked the pages as usual."

Julie accepted the work with a cheerful, "What a week, huh? But at least it's Friday. You know . . ." she said, turning as she was halfway through the doorway, ". . . you should really get married, Marcel. I know you promised your dad that you'd take the magazine to the next level . . . we all promised. But life is short, you know? And it's good to have someone to go home to. Someone who really cares about you."

Marcel smiled and nodded. "I'm working on it."

As soon as the other woman had left the room, Marcel fiddled in her purse for her PDA. Julie wasn't telling her anything that she didn't already know. And something was going to be done about it right now. She had delayed calling Ian all week and had very deliberately avoided him during the two or three attempts he had made to contact her. She hadn't wanted him to think that she desired him as much as she did. But the time for silly pretense was over. She needed what he had so boldly offered her. And, now, she would take it.

Her hands went cold as she picked up the phone and dialed his number. She waited for what seemed an excessive amount of time as the phone rang in her ear. She was just on the verge of hanging up when the ringing ended abruptly with a husky, "Yes?"

The sound of his voice brought a sudden rash of goose pimples to the skin on her arms. And Marcel said in a brisk manner, "This is Marcel."

His voice changed immediately, and the beat of Marcel's heart changed along with it, becoming heavy and thick.

"Marcel Templeton," he said, and there was a definite smile in his voice. "What a nice surprise." And contrarily, he said nothing else.

Marcel released a tight little breath. She'd been hoping that he would take the lead since he definitely knew why it was she was calling. But it would seem that he was going to make her do it.

"Thank you for the lovely roses." And she chewed anxiously on the corner of her lip.

"When I didn't hear from you, I felt maybe I'd chosen the wrong flower."

Marcel cleared her throat. Yes, she should have called to thank him before now, but she had been busy. Very busy. Not everyone in the world had the kind of irresponsible, carefree lifestyle that he did.

"I tried you a couple times." And she cringed inside at the lie. "Then I got kinda busy. But I wanted to call and let you know that I've been thinking about your . . . ah, proposition."

"And you've come to a decision . . . ?"

Marcel wet her lips with the tip of a pink tongue. She had half-expected him to embarrass her by feigning ignorance and forcing her to remind him of his offer. So, his immediate response took her a bit by surprise.

"Yes, I have," she said now. "And I want you to know that if we come to this arrangement, it . . . it will be just that and nothing more. No strings. No ridiculous romance. No promises. No lies."

"OK," he agreed. "And once it's over, we'll just walk away. No tears. No calls. Nothing."

Marcel nodded. "Exactly. And, just for the record, I'm not the kind of woman who breaks down in floods of tears at the drop of a hat. In fact, I never cry. I don't believe in it."

"Is that right? Well, I'm sure that can't be healthy."

Marcel's eyes glittered. "Yes, anyway," she continued, a little anxiously now. "If you'd like to come over tonight, at around sevenish, I could fix dinner."

Ian hesitated for a moment. "Seven tonight? Well, I'll have to rearrange a few things, but . . . OK. Seven is fine." Then he surprised her by asking, "You worked a full day today, didn't you?"

Marcel's brow developed a soft furrow. "Well . . . yes," she answered, wondering where this was going.

He laughed. "Now no need to sound so suspi-

cious. I was about to offer up my services as cook
and bottle washer since I know you must be tired
after a long day of work."

"You cook?" Marcel asked, not even bothering to
conceal the amazement in her voice.

"I don't think you can call me a gourmet chef by
any stretch of the words, but I can take care of myself."

"Well. . . ." Marcel began. She was definitely getting cold feet here. The thought of Ian Michaels in
his tight jeans and an apron was almost more than
she could bear. She was in the mood for a good
dinner, though. But could he actually cook? Or
would she be forced to suffer through a course of
burnt meat and overdone potatoes?

"Come on," he said, and his voice became silky
smooth. "Let me cook for you. It won't be nearly as
bad as you think. And, who knows, you might enjoy
it."

Marcel swallowed hard. What she was really
afraid of was that she might enjoy the entire experience just a little too much.

"All right," she said, and closed her eyes. "What
will you cook?"

"Do you like seafood?" he asked, a pleased note
in his voice.

Marcel's eyes developed a thoughtful glint. Seafood incorrectly done often resulted in very serious
cases of stomach upset. And with all she had on her

plate in the coming weeks, she really could not afford to be laid up for days on end.

"Why don't you try something, ah . . . simple if you really have your heart set on cooking?"

He chuckled. "You can trust me. I do a decent shrimp salad. And white rice. Or would you prefer it with pasta?"

And before she could tell him that if he was really concerned with what she preferred, he would give up the entire idea of cooking altogether, he said, "Actually, the shrimps would go better with pasta and a rich tomato sauce. So, I'll do that this time. OK?" And he laughed again and assured her that she shouldn't worry about a thing. "I'll see you at seven then."

"Seven," Marcel said, and she hung up wondering just what it was she had gotten herself into.

Chapter Twenty

Marcel dressed with great care. She'd arrived home at just before six and gone straight in to take a shower. She'd washed her hair, dried it, and then layered each curl with her favorite fragrance. She had also spent a moment on the scale and had noted with a sense of acceptance that she had gained another two pounds. But she wasn't going to worry about it. Tonight, she was going to get some of her kinks worked out. Maybe, *all* of her kinks worked out.

A little smile touched the corners of her lips and she dabbed some perfume behind an ear. In the past, with her other relationships, she had always held back. Had always been somewhere short of completely uninhibited. There had been certain things that she had always wanted to do. Always wanted to try. But somehow, somewhere in the back of her mind, she'd heard her mother's voice saying, *Nice girls don't do that. Nice girls don't want that. He'll use you and throw you away if you behave like that.* And the voice, until now, had always won. She had curbed her desires, curbed her behavior, curbed everything. But now things were different. She was fully grown now. A woman. And this thing with Ian Michaels didn't matter anyway. So, she could behave in whatever manner she saw fit. And she intended to. Yes. She was going to work óut every little fantasy she had ever had. Now was the time for it. And when the affair had run its course, when they had both had their fill of each other, she would find some nice, decent, completely responsible man to settle down with. And, in the years to come, when she looked back on her younger years, she would remember her crazy little affair with Ian Michaels as just that. A moment of madness. A bit of magic that could never have lasted.

She pulled the hair off her neck and twisted it into a little French roll. Maybe she would wear it up for a change. That would give him a chance to take it down. She closed her eyes and sucked in a luxuriant breath. She'd been having these dreams about his long, thick fingers. She could just imagine the feel of them against her skin. Hard. Gritty. Totally male. He would pull each pin from its resting place, thread his fingers through her hair, massage her scalp.

Maybe run his hands down the length of her neck.
. . . Ah it would be wonderful.

She finished with her hair after deciding to pin it
into an attractive coil with strategically selected tendrils left hanging around the temples and nape of her
neck. Then she spent a minute on her face. Makeup
was something that she only ever wore in modera-
tion. A little lipstick. A touch of foundation. Eyeliner. Maybe on the rare occasion, a little gloss on
her lips. But nothing more elaborate than that. And
even though she wanted the evening to go off without a hitch, she refused to do anything completely
out of character. Using excessive makeup would be
out of character, and so there would be none of that.

At a few minutes before seven, she stepped into
her black crushed velvet dress, smoothed the fabric
over her hips, and then yanked the zipper up in the
back. It was a little on the tight side because of the
weight she had gained, but at least it still fit.

She walked across the room to the mirror and sur-
veyed herself from every possible angle. She
mightn't be able to breathe very well, but she did
look good. And it was the kind of dress that could
be removed with a simple pull on the zipper.

Marcel spent a few minutes out in the tiny sitting
room, arranging pillows, freshening the water in the
solitary glass vase. The stone fireplace, which she
hardly ever used, was stacked with fragrant logs and
the flames were stoked to a low burn. Then a selection of romantic CDs was placed in the CD changer

and the lights dimmed. She considered spreading a thick blanket before the fireplace but decided against it at the last moment. Even though the arrangement between them both would be nothing more than merely a physical one, it still wouldn't do to seem too anxious for things to progress down that inevitable path. She would play it cool until he gave her the signal that he was ready to heat things up. Then. Then . . .

She walked into the kitchen in her clog-heeled sandals and took a quick look around at things. The groceries that she had bought on her way home from the office were already sitting on the side of the sink, the bag of fresh shrimp nicely soaking in a bowl of water, and the pasta poured out of its container and into a jumbo colander. Thick sweet tomatoes and sticks of yellow butter also stood at the ready. Along with two fragrant onions, several pegs of garlic, some basil, and a large container of salt. She would try to make it as easy as possible for him. It wasn't that she didn't believe that men possessed the ability and know-how to cook a good meal. In fact, she readily accepted that some of the best chefs in the world were male. It was just that some perceptive instinct told her that cooking was not one of Ian Michaels's talents. There was nothing about him that suggested that he spent any time at all in the kitchen. It was entirely clear to her that he was accustomed to being waited on hand and foot. The many women in his life were probably more than willing to cater to his every need. They probably fought among themselves over who would be the one to cook for him each day.

Thought shimmered in her eyes. She wasn't sure how she was going to handle the matter of his having other women, since their relationship would be outside the realm of a strictly conventional one. But she wasn't the kind of woman who would put up with the idea of sharing. Regardless. So, she would have to make this clear to him.

The clock on the faux marble mantel chimed on the hour and Marcel glanced at her watch. He was going to be late.

The ringing of the phone just then made her jump. She took a deep breath, walked across the room, and picked up the receiver.

"Marcel, I'm running a little late. I've had a little situation here at home. My niece—she's a bit of a handful." Ian laughed in a rueful manner. "She refused to let me leave. I don't know what I'm going to do about her tantrums. The child has quite a temper. Don't know where she gets it from. Definitely not the Michaels side of the family. Anyway, I'll be there soon. Just didn't want you to worry."

"No problem," Marcel said, smiling. "Take your time." Then, presence of mind made her add, "Are you sure you can make it tonight then?"

"No, no," he assured her. "She's fine now. I spend

most of the day with her, so she's just accustomed to having me around. That's it more than anything else. The baby-sitter has things under control now, though."

"OK, if you're sure," Marcel said again. "Drive carefully."

She hung up and went to sit by the fireside in one of the comfy love seats. The man was a constant surprise . . . a highly pleasant surprise. He was actually . . . considerate. She stared at a burning log. Maybe Tracy was right about her after all. Maybe she did have some unresolved issues when it came to her dealings with men. Was there really more to Ian Michaels than she had originally thought? Had she misjudged him?

She crossed her nicely shaped legs and ran a distracted hand down the length of one ultrasheer-stockinged leg, straightening the hose as she did so. So he had a niece he was obviously raising himself? Not many men would take on the responsibility of raising a young child.

Marcel settled back in the sofa. Nothing he did fit into the behavior pattern of a coldhearted player who pursued and bedded women for fun and profit. It also did not make sense that a selfish, self-centered man would behave so, either. A little smile touched the corners of her mouth. What an absolutely fascinating man Ian Michaels was turning out to be. The more she knew about him, the more she wanted to know.

The sudden flash of headlights in her driveway brought her to her feet. Her heart began to pound in her chest and a warm tide of blood brought a flush to her neck and face. She paused for just a moment to take a deep calming breath, smoothed damp palms over her hips, and then walked to the front door.

Chapter Twenty-One

"For you." And Ian presented her with a large arrangement of velvety red long-stemmed roses.

Marcel met his eyes above the flowers, and hot breath shuddered in her lungs. God, he looked marvelous in his beautifully tailored black slacks and deep navy silk shirt.

"Thank you," she said, gathering the fragrant roses in her arms. Her voice sounded high and breathy, even to her own ears. She stepped back from the doorway and waved him in.

"So everything's OK now with your niece? What's her name . . . ?"

"Daniella," he said, closing the door behind him.

"Let me put these in some water," she said, and hurried into the kitchen. It was silly to feel so nervous around him. He was just a man. A gorgeous, melt-like-butter, sexy man.

She placed the roses in the long glass vase and stepped back to admire them. They were perfect. Just right for the room. Just right for her.

"You look fabulous."

Marcel turned. He was standing with both hands shoved into his pockets, and the hot glint in his eyes brought a fresh stain of blood to her cheeks.

Marcel's eyes darted down the soft velvet stretch dress and then returned to his steady amber-gold eyes.

"It's just an old dress," she said. "I was actually a little nervous about wearing it. I'm not that svelte girl I used to be." She laughed nervously.

Ian's eyes traveled slowly down her body and she suddenly felt light-headed. The man was looking at her as if he wanted to strip her down and feast on her right then and there. And, if the truth be known, if he made a move on her right now, she would do nothing whatsoever to stop him.

When he finally met her eyes again, Marcel's heart was beating as hard as if she had just run a hundred-meter sprint.

He said softly, "You look fine to me."

Marcel's throat clenched. God help her, this man was just too sexy for his own good.

"Come over here."

The blood warmed in her cheeks. "What?"

Instead of repeating the instruction, he shortened the distance between them. He came to stand so close to her that when she breathed, she inhaled the spicy scent of his cologne.

"Don't be afraid of me," he said, and his breath caressed the curve of her cheek.

"I'm . . ." She swallowed. "I'm not afraid of you. Why should I be? Are you dangerous?"

He didn't respond to her attempted light banter. Instead, he lifted a rough palm and stroked the side of her face.

"I want you to know that I will never hurt you." And at that assurance, Marcel met his eyes squarely.

"We agreed earlier that if we decided to do this, there would be no lies between us. I don't want you to make me . . . promises. All I want out of this . . . this thing with you is . . ." She had been about to say "sex," but the expression on his face halted the words in her throat. There was actually a sliver of hurt in his eyes.

"What I mean to say is that there is no need for . . . for any of that. OK?"

But, to Marcel's surprise, he reached for her gently and folded her body close to his. He pressed a warm kiss to the skin just beneath her right eye, another to the tip of her nose, and asked in a voice that held no trace of anger, "Is it so hard to trust? You know, sometimes in life, you've just got to take a chance. It's not a good thing to play it so completely safe all the time. Think of the many things you'll miss out on if you do."

He stroked the curve of her upper lip with his thumb, and then he settled his lips, hot and sweet, on hers.

Marcel shuddered at the raw feel of him and Ian absorbed the shiver, pulling her closer still, fitting her hips snugly to his, moving a hand down to the small of her back to hold her firmly against him.

Almost too soon, it was over and a blend of confusion and hidden fear trembled in Marcel's eyes as Ian lifted his head. She had never known, never known that a simple kiss could be this good. This pure and yet at the same time so very profane.

She tried to speak. Tried to say something intelligible. But words deserted her yet again.

"I'll get dinner started then?"

Marcel nodded and said breathlessly, "Everything's on the counter. I can help if you like?" The words came out in a rush and she stood there in half-embarrassment, looking at him and wondering what in the world she would be like by the end of the evening if a simple kiss had rattled her this much.

His eyes warmed in the most curious manner and he asked, "Has a man ever cooked for you before now?"

Marcel's chin tilted up and the familiar defensive note crept back into her voice.

"No one has ever wanted to before."

"So I'm the first?"

She couldn't see the point of his question. She shrugged. "You're the first. But I don't see why that matters one way or the other."

Ian slid his hands back into his pockets and Marcel was again struck by the expression of power that he gave off completely without effort.

"It matters to me." And he shrugged. "I want to make you happy . . . in a way that no other man has yet."

Marcel just stared at him not knowing what to say. Just who *was* this man?

"You'll find all you need either on the counter or in the fridge," she said again like an idiot. Her brain for the moment had gone into a strange stutter. He wanted to make her happy? OK. OK. He wanted to make her happy. She had never thought that she would ever hear those words from any man. Let alone a man who wanted to be *her* man? It was incredible. Unbelievable. Impossible?

"OK," Ian said, and he began rolling back his long sleeves. "It shouldn't take more than forty-five minutes. So, while I get things ready, you can tell me all about yourself." And he gave her the kind of smile that made her want to smile in return.

Marcel went across to the long sofa and sat. She was beginning to like him. God in heaven, what was she going to do about it? She had told Tracy that things would never get serious. But she had been crazy to say it. Which woman in her right mind would, if given a chance, turn away from a man like Ian Michaels? He was drop-dead gorgeous. He was willing to cook. He had big hands. . . .

"So, I'm ready to hear all about you."

From where she was seated Marcel watched him pick up the bowl of shrimp and empty the water into the sink. She crossed her legs. *What should she tell him?*

"What do you want to know?"

He met her gaze. "Tell me everything."

Chapter Twenty-Two

The smell of something burning yet again drew Marcel from her comfortable spot on the sofa. In the past hour, it had been necessary to put out a small grease fire as the shrimp ignited in a sudden blaze of blue-and-orange flame. Then, not long after that situation had been resolved, several tomatoes, an entire onion, and a chunk of garlic had been reduced to charred and smoking lumps of blackened vegetable flesh. At that point, Marcel had tried to intervene. But Ian had shooed her back to the sofa with the assurance that things were finally under complete control. There was nothing to worry about. He was just a little rusty, that was all. Marcel had watched the unfolding saga with mounting trepidation. At the rate at which he was going, she knew that it would be a miracle if he didn't burn her house to the ground. Then what would she do? She'd be forced to go and live with Tracy, because she had neglected to get herself any fire and water insurance.

"Are you sure I can't do something?" she asked now. And there was a definite thread of nervousness in her voice. If only she had listened to her intuition. She had suspected that he couldn't cook. Why, why in the name of heaven had she agreed to have him try?

"No, no. Everything's fine." And he swore thickly amid a sudden clatter of falling pots. "Go on with your story. You were telling me that your dad started a magazine out here back in the early seventies."

"Yes," Marcel agreed. "He, ah . . . had this vision. . . ." She fanned a hand before her. "You know, I think something else might be catching. Maybe if you turned on the exhaust fan and set the fire to low—"

Something else crashed to the floor and Marcel nodded to herself. It was completely clear that there would be no dinner to be had that night.

"Is it broken?" she asked. She had no idea what had just fallen, but by the sound of it, she guessed that it was not metallic.

"Yes." And there was a slight pause. Then he said, "I think we're going to have to do without the pasta sauce."

"Right," Marcel agreed. "Everything's ready

then?" Her main concern now was getting him out of the kitchen as quickly as was polite.

Ian wiped his hands on a dishcloth. "Well, this isn't exactly what I had intended making. But I seem to have run out of a few things."

"Don't worry about it," Marcel said, and her voice took on a coaxing note. "I'm sure it'll be fine." She wasn't certain of anything of the sort, but over the past two hours she had developed a deep sympathy for him. He had tried so very hard and had succeeded in making an utter and total mess of everything. At the beginning of the evening, she had not been favorably disposed to eating any of his cooking. But now whatever it was he had come up with she would eat and pretend that it was the best thing she had ever tasted.

"Let me dish. You come and sit. You must be exhausted." Breaking and burning almost everything in sight was bound to wear out even the hardiest of souls.

She prepared herself for another round of assurances that he could in fact handle everything himself and was relieved when he agreed, "Yes, I am a little tired. I take my hat off to women. I definitely couldn't go through this every day."

The humor of the entire situation suddenly struck Marcel, and she did her best to control the twitching at the corners of her mouth.

"Come on then. You sit down." And she uncurled

from the sofa and clattered over to the small kitchen. "I'll take over from here."

He gave her a rueful look that made Marcel want to break into gales of laughter. She made a pretense of rubbing a hand across her nose so that he wouldn't see the smile that she was beginning to have great difficulty hiding.

"Don't worry," she said again. "I'm sure everything will taste just fine." And she pressed his hand in a comforting little gesture. His fingers curled immediately around hers, and he brought the hand to his lips and pressed a warm kiss to the center of her palm.

"Tomorrow," he said, "I'll take you out for Mexican. You like Mexican food, don't you?"

Marcel shooed him with a hand. "Go on," she said. "Sit and relax." As long as he wasn't going to try cooking the food, she would agree to almost any meal under the sun. Besides, she really did have a tremendous fondness for burritos and the like.

Once he was seated in the spot she had just vacated herself, Marcel went quickly about the kitchen. The place was a complete wreck. Pots, pans, and dishes overflowed from the sink. And they were all in very bad shape. Burnt bottoms, remnants of nameless vegetables trapped in crusted sauce, broken shards of various dishes.

Marcel held on to a tight sigh. It would take her hours to clear the place up. But the first order of business would be scraping together some semblance of a meal.

She peered into one of the pots on the stove and her heart cringed. How in the world had he managed to get the pasta to that particular consistency? The noodles were like petrified stalks of wheat. And they were quite obviously stuck to the edges and bottom of the pot.

"What do you think of it?" His voice brought her back from her contemplation of the sorry state of the pot.

"Not too bad," she lied bravely. "I should be able to make a meal of it."

How it was she was going to do that she wasn't exactly sure. Maybe if she cut the hard edges off the pasta and whipped up a quick sauce to hide the blackened state of what remained of the shrimp. She could do a green salad, too, if he had left her any tomatoes. . . .

She opened the fridge and peered inside. Lovely. No tomatoes left. But . . . And she rooted around in one of the crisper drawers. There was lettuce. Good. And cucumbers. Thank God he hadn't decided to start on those. There was ranch dressing. And shallots. Green beans and spinach. She could do something with this.

Over the next few minutes, she went about the kitchen like a whirlwind, responding only with short answers to Ian's occasional questions. She chopped the lettuce and spinach, sliced the cucumbers and shallots. Tossed in a handful of green beans cut to just the right size and then prepared her special salad dressing of ranch, vinegar, and shards of tangy cheese.

She scraped the charred shrimp from the pot and arranged as much as she could salvage atop the salad. Then she warmed a loaf of bread and sliced it into generous pieces. She buttered the top slice with golden butter and then arranged the entire loaf in an attractive cascade across a large platter.

"Well, that looks a lot better than what I had originally."

Marcel turned to find Ian almost directly behind her. She had been so engrossed in her attempt to reassemble something edible that she had not heard him come up behind her.

She smiled at him now. "I don't think we're going to be able to do that much with the pasta. Do you have your heart set on having it?"

Their eyes locked, and a warm sensation curled its way around Marcel's heart.

"It's terrible, right?"

"No. Really. It's not that bad. It's just that . . . well, we have a lot of food now. And since we don't have any pasta sauce, because the dish, ah . . . broke . . . we'd have to eat it dry." And Marcel had the sudden urge to stroke the side of his face. He had such very kind eyes. Such deep and thoughtful eyes. How very, very strange.

A smile spread slowly across his face and Marcel's lips curled in response.

"Come here," he said. And he wrapped her in a warm hug and then dropped a quick kiss on her cheek.

"That's really the nicest lie anyone has ever told me. And, just for that," and he touched the tip of her nose with a long index finger, "I'm going to help you set the table."

Marcel swallowed and said hastily, "No. You don't have to. You've done enough." More than enough actually. She really could not afford any more broken dishes.

"I'll handle all of the unbreakables. How about that?"

And the chuckle that Marcel had been holding on to for the longest time bubbled in her chest. She struggled for a moment longer and then let the tide of laughter take her. And he laughed with her, eyes alight with deep humor.

A layer of ice around Marcel's heart cracked a little. It had been a long time since she had shared a genuine moment with a man. And she knew instinctively that this was real. She knew without any doubt that he was not faking, and for some reason unknown to her, it pleased her.

Over dinner, with two twisty white candles burning softly on either end of the table, Ian said with a note of dry self-derision in his voice, "So much for making you happy, huh? And to think that I had planned the entire thing in my mind for days." He gave a brief laugh. "I guess I should have practiced the meal before I opened my big mouth."

"What made you suggest it?" Marcel asked, crunching on a blackened shrimp. And as she waited for his response, she realized in a slightly distracted manner that she hadn't been this happy, this relaxed, in a good long while.

"I wanted to impress you." He placed a forkful of salad into his mouth. "But I guess I failed that particular attempt, miserably. I'm not done with you yet, though." And he gave her an audacious little wink.

Marcel grinned back at him. It was almost inconceivable to her that she was feeling this comfortable with him now when just hours before she had been as nervous as a kitten. But now, she felt as though she could trust him. Almost. She had to remember that she had been down this road many a time before. And always it had led to heartbreak and disillusionment. Would it be different with Ian? She hoped so. She prayed so. He seemed to be such a . . . nice, decent sort of man. So unlike her original impression of him. There was another complication, too. They had both agreed that this relationship between them would not be serious. So, how would she manage to convince him otherwise? And should she really want to? Her heart had been broken so many times before. She was afraid. Afraid to really open herself up again to the possibility of heartache. Because she was beginning to suspect that with very little effort she could come to care deeply about Ian.

"I'm sorry . . . what?" Marcel asked, her eyes flashing back to his. Her mind had drifted for an instant, and she hadn't heard his question.

"These *rules* you were telling me about a little earlier." He paused to sink healthy white teeth into a thick slice of bread. "Are you really serious about them? I mean, do you actually intend to find yourself a man that way?"

Marcel patted her mouth and then said, "Of course I'm serious. You see," she waved a fork to emphasize her point, "they make perfect sense. And any women who're serious about getting married should really do something similar. Because a lot of the confusion and heartbreak that people suffer in the dating game comes from the fact that they're not clear about what it is they want."

"Hmm," Ian agreed. "So, these rules are a way of focusing your attention on the things you think you want in a man?"

"In a nutshell."

"But what happens if a so-called *good* man comes along who's outside of a few of the rules? What happens then? Will you be flexible?"

Marcel took a swallow of white wine and said with a firm note in her voice, "Nope. That's the whole point of having the rules. You don't have to wonder anymore . . . Is this man right for me? Will he be good for me in the long run? The rules help guide you. So flexibility doesn't really come into it."

"So, someone like me—according to your rules— would be out of luck?"

Marcel busied herself with the platter of bread before her. Why in the world was he asking her these particular questions? And how could she possibly answer them without hurting his feelings? And why did he care about her rules anyway?

"Well . . ." She took another moment to consider her words. "It doesn't really matter, does it? I mean, we both want different things . . . ultimately."

"We do?" And his amber eyes appeared thoughtful in the candlelight.

"Yes, of course we do," and she tried to say this with a light note of fun in her voice. She didn't understand what exactly it was that he was after. The kind of relationship that they would have was exactly the kind that most men dreamed of having. No-strings sex. No expectation of a commitment. How much better than that could it get?

"Is your neck a little sore?"

Marcel blinked at him in surprise. "My . . . neck?" Where had that come from now? And, what had made him ask it? She had been going to great pains all evening to conceal the fact that the muscles in her neck were a bit painful.

"Um-hmm." And he scraped back his chair and came around to stand directly behind her. "Now . . ." And both of his hands settled on the base of her neck. "Tell me where."

Marcel swallowed and her heart began to patter in her chest.

"Well . . . here and here," she said, lifting a hand to gently touch the problem spots. And she closed her eyes and tried not to sigh in utter contentment as his hands began to knead in the most divine way. His fingers were big and broad-tipped and so very strong, and he seemed to know exactly the right pressure to apply. Firm enough to relieve the soreness but not so firm that he caused her any discomfort.

In an involuntary little movement, her head drifted gently back to rest against him and she allowed herself the freedom to enjoy every single last minute of it.

His fingers moved over her shoulders and neck like a particularly gifted musician, plucking and massaging away every trace of pain.

When his hands moved down the face of her shoulders to rest on the swell of her bosom, her eyes fluttered back open. A tide of excitement that she could do nothing at all to control rose like molten lava beneath her skin and shimmered there in a hot flush of blood.

Marcel tilted her head back and met his eyes. This was what she had wanted from the very first time their eyes had met. His hands on her, her hands on him.

"Do you want this?"

His voice, so warm, so husky, so very male, caused a run of gooseflesh to rise on the skin of her arms.

"Yes." If only he knew how much she did want it. How much she needed it. She was a strong, independent, passionate woman after all. And she had denied herself for far too long.

He turned the chair toward him, and she watched him with hot eyes.

"Tell me what you want."

Marcel sucked in an unsteady breath. She could hear her mother's voice in her head again, bleating at her. Telling her that these things were only to be enjoyed within the sanctity of marriage. She closed her eyes, reached for his hand, and guided it up the silky length of a thigh. She had wanted exactly this for so long.

He rolled the skirt of the crushed velvet dress back in slow, tantalizing increments, his big fingers stroking higher and higher until they had settled against the soft, wet throbbing point between her thighs.

She made a little sound of encouragement, and in response he parted her legs with consummate skill and settled his mouth against the warm crotch of her silken panties.

Her fingers bunched in his hair as she felt his mouth open against her. His tongue, firm and deliberate, circled the trembling center of her, and she pressed him closer with both hands, pleading in a voice that she could barely recognize as her own, "Take it off. . . . Take everything off."

His teeth gently grazed the delicate nub at the center of her thighs, and Marcel groaned with the impatience of it. He was going too slowly. Too slowly. She wanted him now. Right now.

Her hands went to the waistband of her stockings to pull them lower, but he stayed her with a hand and said, "Not yet."

"But you have to. You must," she said in a jerky manner.

He pulled her firmly toward him and then with his teeth tore a tiny hole in the hose. His tongue darted through the opening, and Marcel clutched at the back of his head and brought him closer to her.

He pushed her lower in the chair and then bent deeper to suckle. A thready "yes" drifted from her lips, and she leaned even farther back to give him better access. Hazy thought flowed like sweet cream through her mind. Why had she never done this before? Taken a lover to tide her over until the right man came along? A man who would give her exactly what she needed and for as long as she needed it.

What good were high ideals in the deep of the night when these passionate needs swept her? But why was he stopping? He couldn't stop now.

Her breath came in scattered bursts and she opened shiny black eyes to find him watching her.

"Now," he said, and his voice was several measures deeper than usual. "What was that first rule?"

Marcel tried to steady her ragged breathing. What? What was he asking her at a time like this? What did it matter what her first rule was? What did anything matter?

"My . . . my first rule?" She barely managed to get the words out.

Ian rubbed the blunt of his thumb against the hot neglected center, and white electricity rattled Marcel from head to toe.

"He must be . . . good in bed."

He moved his thumb again, this time in a delicious little circle, pressing against her with just the right degree of firmness. "I think I can accommodate you on that one."

Marcel almost sobbed in response. She was far too hot to call a halt to things now. If she had been able, she might have considered pulling her skirt back down, getting up, taking a cold shower. But she couldn't. She just couldn't. She was too weak. Far too weak.

He bent to her again, but this time, contrarily, she tried to pull away. But he held her firmly and pleasure in dark unrelenting waves took her. She called his name once, twice, three times. And he growled a response, pulled her closer still, parted each golden pink fold with his tongue, and suckled again, hard and deep.

Marcel's fingers flexed in his hair and she felt a strange blackness begin to close in on her. It was too good. Too intense. But he continued to hold her against him until she began to sob and moan broken words of entreaty. Then and only then did he give her what she wanted . . . needed. Some distant part of her brain registered the snap of his belt buckle, the parting of his zipper, and then he entered her in one solid stroke.

Both eyes sprang open at the feel of him, and her legs lifted to wrap about his waist. And as he moved in that necessary ebb and flow, Marcel's nails curled into the skin of his shoulders, and she urged him on with unintelligible sound, her head thrown back.

Ian lifted her from her perch on the chair and settled her on the floor, never once breaking rhythm. And Marcel held him tighter still. There were tears in her eyes, tears in her throat, tears wrapped in a garland about her heart.

She moved her mouth along the length of his neck and bit. A tiny closing of teeth against smooth, hard flesh. And Ian grunted in supreme satisfaction, removed her legs from about his waist, and bent them back as far as they would go, looping them both about his neck.

Marcel shuddered. Cried out for more, whimpered like a babe when he gave her exactly what it was she needed, and called out to God and all of the saints as it went on and on and on. . . .

Chapter Twenty-Three

The remainder of the night was passed in a similar manner. And it was only at about three in the morning that they both retired to the comfort of Marcel's queen-size bed. Then and only then did she rest. And it was some of the most peaceful sleep she had yet experienced. Lying against the flat of his chest, her head tucked perfectly beneath his chin, she allowed herself to slip into full-blown contentment.

Later, just as the first blush of sunlight stained the sky pink, she climbed atop him and greeted the day with sweet pleasure coursing through her. She fell into slumber again after that, and Ian held her as she slept, his eyes narrowed to golden slits. He had never had such a time with a woman as the night he had just passed. Marcel had been even more passionate than he had imagined. She was an amazing woman and he would not allow another to have her until he had had his fill of her. For some reason not yet clear to him, he wanted to ferret out all of her many broken parts and put them back together so that she no longer hurt. She had touched some deeper part of him. Why? How? He did not understand. But he did know that he would thwart any attempts she made to date other men. She was his. Completely. For now.

Ian stroked the flat of his palm across a smooth brown shoulder and watched with gentle amusement as a little frown flickered across her brow. She was such an enigma. But he would figure her out. He would crack the code. There was a little problem, though. One that could potentially unravel the tentative trust she had obviously placed in him. She didn't know who he was. Didn't know that his company was the one currently making aggressive moves toward her magazine. He had not known it himself until she had told him the story about her father and his magazine. *La Beau Monde.*

He slung a long leg across her and pulled her closer to him. He would have to tread very carefully, and when she trusted him fully he would explain everything to her. And if he was lucky, she would accept that his decision to keep quiet had been for the best.

Marcel opened a sleepy eye and stretched in a long and feline manner against his chest. She looked up to find that he was wide awake and watching her.

"Hi," she said, smiling. She felt different. Vibrant. Reborn somehow. What a difference a long night of fantastic lovemaking could make.

Ian leaned forward to kiss her warmly and Marcel savored the moment, stroking a hand down the side of his face. It was so wonderful to have a man in her bed again. A real man.

"Ready for some breakfast?"

Marcel chuckled. "You're not going to cook it yourself, are you?"

His husky laugh reverberated in the room, and Marcel beamed at him. God, she just couldn't believe it. She was happy. And it felt great. It was as though she could take on the entire world. Handle whatever life threw at her. Was it just that she was still wrapped in the warm blanket of afterglow? Or was it real?

She was reluctant to remove herself from his embrace, but she knew that if they remained as they were for very much longer, they might very well end up spending the entire day in bed.

Ian caught at her hand as she attempted to leave the bed, and for just a moment she allowed him to hold it.

"Don't leave."

She laced her fingers with his and tried to be firm. "If I don't get up now, I won't get anything at all done today."

He shifted so that his head rested on the flat of his palms.

"It's Sunday," he said. "A day made for just lazing around. What do you have to do today that's more important than that?"

She stepped into her robe and wound the ties about her waist.

"Well, I've got to clear up the kitchen, for one."

"I'll help you with that."

Marcel shook her head and a playful little smile touched the corners of her mouth.

"I don't know if I can afford it."

He laughed. "I'm sorry about that. I'll replace everything I damaged."

Marcel shushed him with a hand. "Don't worry about it," she said now. "I needed some new dishes anyway."

"Well, what can I do then?"

Their eyes locked, and hidden devilry lit simultaneously in both pairs of eyes.

"Behave," she said, but her heart warmed at the expression on his face. It made her feel good, whole, complete to know that the experience they had shared had not simply been good for her.

"Are you sure that's what you want?" And he made a sudden and totally unexpected lunge for her. Marcel dodged his outstretched arm, but he pursued. And she was forced to skitter around the foot of the bed and plead with an outstretched arm.

"Come on, Ian. Really. I have things to do."

But he followed her, and Marcel was forced to turn tail and run for the bathroom, shrieking all the way. She barely managed to slam and lock the door before he caught up with her. She rested against the whitewashed wood with a hand pressed to her chest. God, she felt just like a schoolgirl. It had been years, simply years, since she had experienced this rush of emotion. Her heart was beating fit to break, and she felt almost giddy. And yes, the strange glow that she was feeling was happiness. Happiness. He had promised to make her happy, and lord if he hadn't somehow managed to do just that.

She bathed and dressed quickly, then allowed him to do the same. When he emerged from the bathroom with a too-short towel wrapped about his waist, water dripping from his hair, Marcel watched him with admiring eyes. He was a magnificent specimen of manhood. Broad shoulders. Long, muscular torso. Hard, strong legs. He was a beauty. There was no doubt about it.

"I'm going to check in on Daniella," he called to her from the bedroom.

"She'll be wondering where you are," Marcel said. "Are you sure she's OK for this length of time with just the baby-sitter?"

"Vera's one of the most reliable people I know."

And Marcel was left to ponder on that little comment as she cracked and fried eggs, made golden slices of buttered toast, and brewed a pot of steaming hot black coffee. Who was Vera? An old girlfriend? Someone who was only too willing to drop everything whenever he asked her to?

She put two place mats down on the table and then brought out the food. She heard his voice as she walked back and forth between kitchen and little dining room, and she did her best not to listen, but every so often a snatch of words would catch her attention. And she noted with a slight frown between her eyes that he was obviously deeply fond of this Vera person, whoever she was.

"I hope you like eggs," she called as soon as it was apparent that he was no longer on the phone.

"Whatever you cook for me is fine." He appeared in the doorway bare-chested, clothed only in a pair of pants. And Marcel stood firmly on the warm sensation that stole into the corner of her heart. He looked so much as though he belonged right there with her.

She blinked and tried to focus. She had to stop being so fanciful; if she didn't, she would never survive the relationship. And even worse, she might decide to abandon her rules. And if that happened, she would be lost.

"Your hair's still wet." It was an unnecessary comment because obviously he had not yet finished dressing. But the sight of his broad, smooth chest and tight, trim waist was almost enough to make her reconsider her decision to spend the day out of bed.

And, almost as though he had anticipated those very thoughts, he came across to her now and stood looking at her with the gaze of a particularly well satisfied lion.

"Are you sure you won't consider coming back to bed?"

Marcel pulled out her chair and sat. Much more of this and she would.

"I told you all about myself last night. Now it's your turn," she said, pushing the brimming plate of toast toward him. She thought to distract him with chatter, but she could tell by the gleaming look in his eyes that she hadn't been at all successful in that regard.

He pulled out the facing chair and sat, too. He helped himself to toast, poured them both mugs of coffee, and then said, "My life so far has been very . . . normal. Not nearly as interesting as your own." And he flashed her a smile that didn't fool Marcel for a second. She recognized evasion when she saw it. He obviously did not want to talk about himself. Why was that? Was he so very ashamed of who he was? Of what he did?

"No, no," and her voice became deliberately play-ful. "You don't get off that easy, mister. Your life can't be that uninteresting." And she waved a piece of toast at him. "Like for instance, why are you the one taking care of your niece . . . you, a single man?

Where's her mother? Better yet, where's her father?"

A flicker of emotion appeared for an instant in his eyes and then disappeared as quickly. And Marcel was immediately sorry she had brought the subject up.

"You don't have to talk about it if you don't want to." And she reached across to hold one of his hands.

"No. It's fine." He bent his head to take a sip of coffee. "Daniella is my younger brother's daughter. He passed away a couple years ago."

Marcel's small sound of sympathy was met with a steady-eyed glance that betrayed no answering emotion.

"I'm all she has, really. Her mother . . . well, let's just say her life isn't stable enough. She can barely manage to take care of herself from day to day. It's not the right kind of life for a little child."

"But she has you. And that's a good thing," Marcel said. And she realized as she uttered the words that she really believed them. There were unseen layers to this man that she had completely failed to notice before.

He nodded. "Yes, she does." And they exchanged a smile.

They fell into an easy conversation after that. He told her about growing up on the streets of Brooklyn, New York. About bouncing around from one foster home to the next. About the time when he and his brother had hitchhiked all the way cross-country to

California just so they could spend the summer on the beach. He told her about the things they had done for money.

He laughed in a rueful manner. "There's nothing we didn't do. I mean, nothing really outside the law, but we had a good time."

"Did your brother look like you?"

He scratched the side of his neck and the light of memory lit in the backs of his eyes.

"We were about the same height and build. Different eyes, though. His were dark. We used to compete with each other, you know. Anything I did, he wanted to do better or longer . . . or bigger. We used to have these wonderful dreams. We were going to conquer the world. Make everything all right for the little people."

Marcel rubbed a finger beneath her nose, because for some curious reason, she felt like crying. He had loved his brother deeply. That much was evident. And, by some cruel stroke of fate, the one person who had always been there, the one person who really mattered, had been taken away.

"But you shouldn't give up on your dreams, though," she said now. And she reached across the table again to give his arm a little squeeze. "You can still do it. You're still young."

"Thirty-nine," he said in a dry manner. "Not so very young anymore."

"Well," she countered. "It's not eighty-nine. You

still have the best years of your life ahead. Just imagine what you might be able to do, with the right woman at your side."

She hadn't been speaking of herself, of course, but she could tell by the quick little glance he gave her that he thought that she was perhaps giving him some kind of a hint.

"I wasn't talking about me," she hastened to clear it up, lest he misunderstand her.

He chuckled. "That never occurred to me for a second. I know you don't want me. I don't fit your rules."

"That's true." And she said this with a pensive expression in her eyes.

"Well, we can't have everything in life, I guess. But," and his eyes took on a wicked expression, "we can have some things."

And before Marcel could even think to avoid him, he was out of his chair. She managed one startled, "Ian, no." But her protests were futile. He scooped her from her seat in such an effortless manner that Marcel could only marvel at the strength that it must have taken to do it. She was plump, after all. At least twenty-five pounds above her ideal weight.

She managed one final protest when her back touched the soft mattress. But he brushed every trace of resistance away with a line of feather-soft kisses that began at the base of her neck and wound its way down the flat of her stomach to the wet point between her legs.

Much later, as she cuddled in his arms with the heat of the day upon them, he said, "So, do you still feel like Mexican tonight?" And he turned onto his side to look directly into her eyes. "Or do you feel like something else?"

She played with one of his hands, and at the back of her mind Tracy's rule about the size and thickness of a man's fingers brought a smile to her face. It was so very true.

"Mexican sounds perfect. There's a really nice restaurant just outside the city. They're right on the ocean. We can sit on the terrace and actually see the waves break on the beach. And . . ." She beamed at him. "They serve the best chimichangas I've ever tasted."

"Well, I'll have to take you to that one later. Tonight, though," and he leaned in to kiss her mouth, "tonight, I'm going to take you to what I'm sure is the best Mexican restaurant in the entire world."

Marcel propped her head on the flat of a palm. She felt so foolishly happy.

"This I've got to see," she said, a cheeky note in her voice. "Because let me tell you, La Mexicana is legendary around here."

He touched her nose with a finger. "I promise you, I can top that. After the kind of meal I prepared last night, I'd better do something special. You know what I mean?"

Marcel laughed heartily. He was so funny. So interesting. So strangely nice. She didn't have the heart to tell him that if he was really going to top La Mexicana, he would probably have to break the bank to do it. The restaurant was definitely high-end. A celebrity hangout, no less. And at least once or twice a year, it was written up in various gourmet and other fine dining magazines.

"Well, we'll see," she said, still smiling.

Chapter Twenty-Four

And later that evening with the heat of the day burnt to a measured chill, she prepared with great care. An hour spent soaking in the tub. Another fifteen minutes creaming and perfuming every inch of skin. Then, her hair, worn this time in loose flowing waves about her shoulders.

Ian had left around mid-afternoon, promising to return to pick her up at six o'clock. His parting comment that she bring a sweater and a change of clothing had made her wonder exactly what it was he was planning. But she spent no more than a few minutes puzzling over the entire thing. He was probably planning a little walk along the beach after dinner with some sinful lovemaking down in the sand to close out the evening. And, really, if that was it, she couldn't be more pleased. He was definitely, without question, the best lover she had ever had. He was gentle, firm, patient, skilled, vigorous. And his stamina. That was another matter entirely. She could only imagine what he must have been like as a younger man if at thirty-nine he could go for simply hours on end.

She was still brimming with good humor when the phone began to ring at just after five. She snatched it from its resting place and almost purred a pleasant, "Hello?"

The voice on the other end sounded just as pleased. "Hello yourself. So, how'd your hot little night go?"

"Tracy," Marcel gushed. "All I can say is . . . oh . . . my . . . God. You know what I'm talking about? That man has some very serious skills."

And she passed the next several minutes filling Tracy in on some of the more interesting parts of the previous evening.

"And he's taking me out to dinner tonight, girl," she said, sounding just as pleased as punch about it. "So, you know I can't talk too long. But sometime this week I'll come over. OK?"

She listened to Tracy's smug *I told you so*s with a completely different level of tolerance. It was so incredible what the love of a good man could do. She blinked at that thought. She really was getting ahead of herself.

"I promise I'll come by this week," Marcel said

again as Tracy complained that she probably wouldn't even show up now that she was so involved with her little fling.

She hung up after a minute more and went back to sit before the mirror. She was going to wear something more casual tonight. Dressy jeans. A wispy blouse with hidden silver threads. High-heeled sandals. Not her favorite type of shoe heel, but she would try to struggle along. She would take a heavy sweater, too, just in case her suspicion about the walk along the beach was right.

She weighed herself faithfully just before pulling on the black jeans. One entire pound gone. She closed her eyes. Thank the lord, things were looking up.

Evening came with silky quiet, and Marcel stood at her bedroom window watching the play of colors with thoughtful eyes. Soft pink edged with splashes of red. An artist's stroke of white. A dash of blue. Slowly creeping indigo. And the sun, sinking beyond the horizon clothed in golden contentment.

The beauty of the night had begun its inevitable journey across the sky, and an intoxicating little breeze blowing in from the face of the ocean paused to pull at the feather-soft ends of Marcel's hair. She brushed a swatch out of her eyes and looked toward the road with barely concealed excitement. The chug of an old motor. It had to be Ian's truck.

She turned to get the shoulder bag that sat at the foot of the bed. She had packed a few things. A beach towel for the sand. Men never seemed to think of the really practical things. She'd also included a thick oatmeal sweater. A sweatshirt. And fresh underwear.

She picked up the bag now and went back to the window.

"I'll be right down." She waved. And she quickly pulled the window in, secured the latch, and then ran a quick check. The hot comb was off. So were the iron and the stove. Perfect. She was all ready to go.

She clipped smartly down the short flight of stairs to the door and tried her level best not to let the deep excitement she was feeling show.

He was on the doorstep when she pulled back the door, and he was simply gorgeous. Dressed as she was. Stonewashed jeans that clung in the most amazing way to his long, muscular legs. A black long-sleeved shirt, rolled at the wrists. Sneakers.

"You look beautiful."

His eyes glowed a warm amber in the fading daylight. And Marcel, in a completely uncharacteristic gesture, responded to his compliment by kissing him lightly on one cheek.

"You look pretty fantastic yourself, sir."

He laughed in a manner that made Marcel feel warm all over. She closed and locked the door behind her and tossed the key into her clutch purse, then turned to him with a saucy little look.

"Well, I'm good and hungry for anything you might have in mind."

He took her hand in his and bent to press a quick kiss to the tip of her nose.

"I like a direct woman," and he winked at her.

He handed her into the truck, shut the door, and then walked around to the driver's side and got in. The engine started without considerable effort, and once they were on their way, he turned to her with an enigmatic look.

"So, just how hungry are you?"

Marcel couldn't help but chuckle at the wicked expression on his face. She knew exactly what he meant.

"You're terrible, you know that? Are you sure you're thirty-nine? I thought men were supposed to slow down with age?"

He lifted a deliberate eyebrow. "*I* was talking about food. What did you think I meant?"

Marcel grinned at him. "Right." She looked at him for a long moment. "So," she said slowly, "tell me why it is that you're not married yet. I've only spent twenty-four, twenty-eight hours with you, and already I like you. What's the matter with all of the women out there? Are they all crazy?"

"You like me?"

She met eyes gone golden in the twilight and

smiled. "You're very likable. I couldn't have been more wrong about you."

A pleased expression came over his face. "Well, it's never a good idea to make instant judgments about people. They almost always turn out to be wrong."

He allowed that comment to settle before asking, "Did you remember to bring a change of clothes?"·

"You're being so secretive about this dinner. Where are we going? La Jolla?"

He smiled. "Don't you like surprises?"

And she was forced to be content with that response until they had taken the third exit ramp off the freeway.

"Oh," she said now. "We're going to La Quintana." She gave him a look of approval. "You're right, the food there is good. My friend Tracy and I go there all the time. You remember Tracy, right?" And she chatted nicely about her friend until it became apparent that they had driven right past the turnoff for the restaurant. She turned behind to look and then said, "I think we missed the turn back there. But you can make a U-turn up here and—"

"We're not going there."

They were bumping down a little dirt road now and Marcel shielded her eyes against the fading sun.

"But there's nothing out here."

He turned off onto a black-topped road that seemed to suddenly appear out of nowhere. Marcel went completely silent as the airfield appeared around a bend in the road. Her brain churned through various possibilities, and as the reality of things became clearer, a little sigh bloomed in her chest. He had probably cooked something else for them. That was it. He had cooked something else and had planned a rustic little picnic out by the airfield. He probably thought it would be fun to eat and watch the planes as they flew over. There were a few things he hadn't considered, though. Things like the noise. The dirt. And also the fact that they might not be allowed to picnic there.

Ian pulled the truck up to a little chain-link gate, and Marcel said in a slightly alarmed manner, "Ian, I don't think we can go in there. It looks private."

"Don't worry," he assured her. "I know somebody here."

And before she could respond to that, the gate was being opened and they were through it. He pulled the truck into an empty spot, cut the engine, and turned to her with, "Well, we're here."

Marcel nodded. It was as she had thought. They were to dine on a selection of burnt burritos, singed tacos, and only God alone knew what else. But where it was they were going to do that was completely beyond her.

"Did you bring a table?" she asked.

He opened the door and got out. "We're not going to need one."

And he came around to help her down. "Everything should be ready for us, I think."

He took her elbow and walked her quickly toward an approaching man, and as the man came toward them, the first niggle of concern raised its head in Marcel's mind. It was as clear as day. They were going to be thrown out.

She gripped his arm. "Ian, I don't think this is such a good idea."

The man was upon them now, and Ian nodded at him and said, "Everything all set?"

And the man, who to Marcel's keen eye looked more like a bodybuilder than anything else, returned the nod and said, "The plane's waiting."

Marcel's eyes darted from the man's face to Ian's and then back to the man. What was going on? He hadn't chartered a small plane for a little trip around San Diego before dinner, had he? The cost would be unbelievable. She attempted to intervene again.

"Ian, maybe we shouldn't do anything elaborate before dinner."

But all he said was, "Trust me. OK?" And then led her quickly past a collection of small twin-engines out onto the airstrip. Marcel's heart went cold as it became apparent that they were heading toward a sleek-nosed Learjet. The steps lowered as they approached, and Ian wrapped an arm about her.

"Up you go."

Marcel walked up the shiny stairs with knees that

had begun to shake just a little. Had she been right about Ian? Was he involved in something illegal? What was this plane? And why were they getting aboard? They were obviously the only passengers, too.

She stepped into the belly of plush luxury. Tan leather seats. Shiny tables between the chairs. Soft cream carpeting. Vases of red roses everywhere.

Marcel blinked at the woman who was standing before her and said in a bald manner, "What?"

The woman smiled and said again, "I was wondering if you would like a glass of champagne, miss?"

Marcel looked at Ian, and for the life of her she couldn't understand why it was he was so very calm about everything.

"I . . . suppose some champagne might be nice."

She sank into one of the soft leather chairs, and Ian selected a solitary long-stemmed rose and then seated himself right next to her.

"This," he said, "is for you. And also, all of these, too." He pointed to the many beautiful long-necked vases that were carefully positioned about the cabin.

Marcel took the flower with numb fingers and, because her brain was still reeling, completely forgot to thank him for it. "We're going to . . . to have dinner in here?"

Ian leaned across to buckle her seatbelt. "No, we're going to have dinner in Mexico. I promised you I'd take you out for some Mexican food. The real thing."

She gripped his forearm, nails biting into his skin.

"Mexico? But . . . how? Who goes to Mexico just for dinner? I mean—" She massaged her temples and tried her best to think straight. "How did you get this plane?" And then she asked the fearful question trembling in her breast. "Ian, tell me the truth: what exactly do you do for a living?" He was a smuggler, A gunrunner or, God Almighty, worse!

"The plane's not mine," he said in a consoling manner. "It belongs to the corporation I work for. It's a corporate jet. Used to fly senior executives from point A to point B, at a moment's notice."

"You're a . . . businessman?"

He nodded. "Yes."

Marcel absorbed the short answer in silence. Yes. He was a businessman. And a senior one, too, by the looks of things. Why had that possibility never occurred to her? But why would she have thought it of him? There was nothing, absolutely nothing, about him that said "businessman." He drove around town in a very shabby old truck, after all. Didn't appear to work regular hours. Was he telling her the truth?

"What kind of business are you in?"

He snapped the belt around his waist as the plane began its slow taxi.

"Television. Radio. That sort of thing. But," and

he reached for one of her hands, "will you promise me one thing?"

She looked at him with eyes that were not exactly trusting.

"Depends on what that one thing is."

He touched her chin with an index finger, and silver electricity rattled her.

"Trust me. Please?"

She nodded. OK. She didn't trust men that easily. But OK. She would give it a try. She would try.

"We won't talk about work, either. Promise?"

And for the remainder of the evening, she kept the promise. They arrived in Cancun just after dark, and Marcel watched the descent into the city with the eyes of a child. The lights of the resort city were spread out for miles in a wonderful tapestry of white, some blinking in and out, others steady, but all beautiful. Tears gathered in Marcel's throat as she watched it all from her place beside the window. It wasn't that she had never traveled before. She had. A few years before, she had gone to the Bahamas. And before that, she had spent a weekend in Las Vegas. But no one, no one, had ever even thought to do anything so wonderful, so special, for her.

So when she felt his warm lips brush across her cheek, she turned and gave him a slow, deep kiss. When he deepened it even further, she felt the prick of tears at the backs of her eyes. Later, she realized that never before in her adult life had she been wined, dined, and romanced in such a manner. Ian had pulled out all the stops. A limousine waiting at the airport to whisk them away to dinner on the sands of a private beach. The curl of the ocean lapping around the legs of the table. Strolling guitarists strumming softly melodic Mexican love songs. Dancing in the waves. Getting soaking wet but not caring at all. Dining on specially prepared dishes, all of her favorites. Holding hands. Laughing at the call of the wind . . .

It had been a night for the record books and Marcel's heart had shuddered every time she looked into his eyes. They had changed clothes after dinner and passed the next several hours lying in the sand doing nothing more than counting the stars and talking.

Marcel had not wanted the evening to end. Had prayed that it not end. But it had. And on the flight back to San Diego, she had fallen asleep in Ian's arms filled to the brim with happiness.

Chapter Twenty-Five

Monday morning came too soon and Marcel remained in bed a full hour longer than was her normal practice. She had arrived home in the wee hours of the morning, tumbled right into bed, and passed the rest of the night wrapped in sweet slumber.

The insistent pealing of the front doorbell at ten o'clock in the morning finally pulled her from beneath the covers. She squinted sleepy eyes at the face of her watch and then dragged herself upright. She had overslept. Something she had not done in years, but who could blame her? She had had simply the most magical weekend. It had not occurred to her even once that she would have so enjoyed Ian's company. But she had. He was such an interesting person. And even though she had vowed never to like him, she couldn't help it. She did.

"Coming, I'm coming!" she bellowed to the person who had his finger on the bell. She wrapped herself quickly in the robe lying at the foot of the bed, stopped before the mirror to run a quick comb through her hair, and then hustled out to the front door. She checked the peephole, and for just a second her heart shimmied in her chest. A part of her had been hoping that it was Ian.

She pulled back the door.

"Yes?"

The man on the doorstep shoved a clipboard at her and said, "Quick Response messenger service, ma'am. Special delivery. Sign here please." And he tapped a spot on the page.

Marcel took the pen, signed, and then retired indoors again to inspect the envelope. It was from her assistant, Julie. She walked across to the wraparound bar and sat on one of the stools, her mind already in overdrive. Usually Julie only sent a messenger out to the house if it was something of great importance. But why hadn't she called her first?

Her eyes went to where the phone sat and to the answering machine. The message light was on. Julie had called after all.

Marcel tore the letter open and peered inside. She pulled out the handwritten note and read it once, and then again. Then she reached into the little packet for the *San Diego Business* magazine. It was an advance copy, scheduled to hit the newsstands in two weeks. Her fingers shook a little as she whipped quickly to the page indicated in the note.

She covered her mouth with her hand. Oh, God in heaven, it couldn't be. In the features section, dressed in his characteristic jeans and T-shirt getup, looking just as cool as you please, was the man she had just spent the entire weekend and a good part of the previous night with.

Her index finger raced to the highlighted box showing all of Tyson's recent acquisition. There were half a dozen magazines listed. And at the very bottom, "the latest on the list, and the focus of all his considerable attention," was *La Beau Monde*. "Will this crown jewel be an addition to the Tyson Media empire by the end of the month?" the article asked.

She slipped the paper back into the envelope. She felt cold and hot at the same time. So, that had been the reason for his relentless pursuit of her. He had been after her magazine all along. She was such a fool, such a blind fool, for not seeing it. His strong interest in her had made her suspicious, of course. But because of his good looks she had misjudged him. She had made the very mistake that men had been making for centuries. Pretty face. Empty head. Not true. Not true. No wonder she had thought that he carried himself like a man of power. And that would explain the corporate jet and everything else. He was the CEO. The chairman of the board. The owner of Tyson Media, the very company her own father had warned her against.

She got off the stool and took a little turn about the small sitting room. Everything. Everything had been a lie. Some little part of her heart had actually wanted to believe that he actually liked her. But it had all been a lie. One big act. Just an elaborate pretense so that he might get his hands on her magazine. That was the reason he had pulled out all the stops this past weekend. But he had made his little announcement too soon. The nerve of the man. She had met some characters in her time, but he was the coldest, most deliberate bastard she had yet come across.

She wiped her eyes with a terry cloth sleeve. Why was she crying? It was stupid. She had always known that he would betray her in the end. It had just happened sooner, rather than later. It was her fault entirely for trusting him. For not listening to her instincts. To her rules. But all wasn't lost. He didn't know that she knew who he was yet. Didn't know that she was aware now of what he was up to. So she would turn the tables on him. She would show him that he had decided to tangle with the wrong person.

She went to sit on the stool again and wiped an angry hand across the side of her face. Why was she still crying? It wasn't as though she was in love with the man or anything like that. No one in her right mind fell in love with anyone else in just forty-eight hours. It was impossible. Ridiculous. And she wouldn't be the first one to do it. She would make him love her, though. She would do it in as deliberate a fashion as he had tried to do with her. Then, she would leave him. And she would do so without a single ounce of pity. It was just a sad state of affairs that she couldn't take his company away from him. And to think she had believed his sob story about his brother and niece. How he must have laughed at her. If he'd ever had a brother or a niece, there was probably no love lost between them at all.

Marcel reached forward and stabbed the playback button on the answering machine. Now, it would be her turn to laugh. Her turn to inflict some damage. And after she was finished with Mr. Ian Michaels, after her magazine was safe, she would take a vacation. Far away from people. Far away from life. Maybe a nice cruise. To Mexico. A frown settled in the backs of her eyes. No, not there. She might never go there again. Maybe the Caribbean. Somewhere beautiful and warm where there was a lot of blue water and nothing but bright and peaceful skies.

Chapter Twenty-Six

Hours and a tub of ice cream later, Marcel decided to listen to her remaining messages. Not that there was much point, since she didn't care about much except maybe castrating Ian Michaels. But that little red light had kept blinking, blinking at her, as if obsessively trying to warn her of danger ahead. And frankly, she didn't think she could handle any more surprises. But nothing could be any worse than what Ian had done to her? Right?

She inhaled deeply and pressed the play button. There was a message from Tracy. She wasn't going to *believe* what had happened. Never in a million years would she believe who Ian Michaels really was.

The next message was from Bill Cook, and Marcel's finger went straight to the erase button. These were the kinds of men she had to choose from. Crazy. Cold-hearted. Immoral. Deceitful. All bastards.

But it was the next message that had her sitting up straight, empty ice cream carton tumbling off her lap and rolling across the floor. Her mother's voice, just as chipper as ever, said, "Honey girl, I'm coming to help. Call it a working visit. I'll explain when I get there, OK?"

Marcel listened to the rest of the message with fear in her eyes. Oh, God Almighty, a working visit. *What did that mean?* And she was arriving that very day on the early morning flight from New York.

This day had just gotten a whole lot worse.

Marcel stood in her living room and saw nothing but a potential disaster. She'd been so involved with Ian—*the creep*—these last several days that she hadn't had the time to do any cleaning. And in preparing for her date last evening she had removed a substantial number of clothes from the closet. There were things sitting in little unsorted piles on various chairs. Shoes, belts, garters, and lord knows what else scattered all about the floor. There were the dishes from Ian's disastrous attempt at dinner still in the kitchen sink. The shower hadn't been properly scrubbed in days. Or was it weeks? And she hadn't done any laundry at all in a good long while.

She sprang from the bar stool and made a beeline for the bedroom. It wasn't that she was a slob. She wasn't. She loved nothing better than a nice, clean place. She had just let things slide a little bit this weekend. Besides, she had so much stuff going on. The magazine. Trying to beat her biological clock. It was all hard, hard work. Especially when the men she kept running into were bums and completely intent on giving her absolutely no help whatsoever. She was completely sure that Ian Michaels wouldn't care two hangs if she should die childless and alone. All he cared about apparently was getting his hands on her poor father's magazine.

She began scooping clothes from her bed and carting the piles across to the little walk-in closet in the corner of the room. There wasn't enough time to spend in folding anything. Her mother could arrive at any moment. And if she did arrive to discover everything in such an awful mess, there would no end to the self-recriminations, crying, and only the good lord knew what else.

For the next half an hour, Marcel darted about like a whirlwind, scooping things up, tossing them in closets, drawers, behind doors, under her bed, and every other conceivable place. She was sweating and out of breath at the end of it all but had managed to accomplish part of the cleanup effort. She slapped a shower cap on her head next and went in with bucket, scrubbers, and mop to tackle the bathroom.

As she mopped and buffed, scrubbed and scraped, she muttered peevishly to herself. The old truism about a woman's work never being done needed an instant update. A woman's work was never done because a woman's life was pure hell. Plain and simple. Men really didn't understand how very easy they had it. All they had to do was wake in the morning, eat, and then go off to work. What did they know about suffering? About menopause? About the agonies of labor and childbirth? What did they really know about any of those things? And of course they were all completely clueless about the bunions, carbuncles, and other deformities that came from shoving pairs of feet into unnaturally high heels just to attract men. Then . . . and she paused in her ramblings to wipe a soapy hand across her brow. Then they had the absolute nerve to go out and start making movies like *Boomerang* and the like, which made jokes about the poor women who ended up with lumpy Frankenstein feet for all of their trouble.

She yanked back the shower door and glared at the tub. If things were completely up to her, men would be required to spend at least half an hour a day, every day, down on their hands and knees, buffing and scrubbing things. Then they might get a smidgen of understanding about what life was all about. What so-called "women's work" was all about. Why didn't they ever ask her about it? She would tell them all. Willingly. It was hell. Nothing else. Just hell. Pure and simple.

She squirted some Soft Scrub into the bath and groaned as her back made a cracking noise as she bent over. Look at that. She was getting arthritis, too. She could just feel it beginning to creep all the way down her spine. Soon her knees, ankles, and fingers would be all messed up. And if things continued at their current rate of deterioration, she probably wouldn't even be able to bend her hips properly on her wedding night. And then what would happen? Her husband would think she was frigid, and the wastrel would go off with some buxom eighteen-year-old who could peel a grape with the cheeks of her firm behind.

She rubbed at the tile for ten entire minutes more, paying particular attention to the discolored ring of soap scum that had somehow accumulated around the mouth of the bathtub.

Finally she sat back on her heels to survey her handiwork. Well, it didn't look as though anything else was going to come off. If her mother didn't think that was clean enough, it was just too bad. It was definitely as clean as it was going to get tonight.

She straightened from her kneeling position with some difficulty and placed both hands against the small of her back. Lord, what she wouldn't do right then for a good old-fashioned back rub. What she needed, really needed, was a man with good, strong hands. Good, thick fingers. A callus or two here and there just for added character. What she needed was a man like . . . No. She stood firmly on the thought. No, she didn't want him. She didn't want Ian Michaels. So what if he was good in bed? So what if he had made her the happiest that she had perhaps ever been?

She massaged her back and then bent to retrieve the mop and bucket. God in heaven, why couldn't she find herself a good man? All she wanted was one who didn't have major personality problems. Or one who wasn't likely to get her killed on a freeway during a police chase. Or arrested for lewd conduct in a public place. And definitely not someone who would, at her trial, as she was staring a possibly stiff sentence behind bars right in the teeth, just brush the whole incident off by consoling her with the assurance that she shouldn't worry about a single little thing, because he would be making a very good offer for her magazine.

Marcel trundled out to the kitchen with the beginnings of self-pity shining brightly in her eyes. Was it too much to ask that there be just one normal man left in the world? One normal man that she could have? She rubbed the side of her face with a shoulder. No matter how bleak things might appear, though, she wouldn't cry anymore. She had awoken in such high spirits, but now she felt tired. Tired, confused, and completely stressed out. She had to stay focused, though. With her mother arriving and Ian Michaels showing his true colors so very soon, she had to.

She turned the hot water tap on the dishes and then gave her robe a glance. Maybe she should change into one with slightly shorter sleeves. One of her old ones maybe. There was no point in getting this one all wet and grimy just for the sake of a few dishes. She'd had it for a whole year, and with a little care it would serve her for many more years, too.

She was in and out of the bedroom within minutes, having neatly placed the attractive pink-and-white-striped robe on a padded hanger and left it conveniently hanging over a twisted lump of clothes on the floor of the closet. On her feet she wore her comfortable but slightly ratty terry cloth slippers. She spent a moment putting an industrial-size knot in the belt about her waist, adjusted the shower cap on her head so that it sat more comfortably, and then went across to the sink to begin work on the dishes. She was right in the middle of pouring a good quantity of detergent into the pouch on the dishwasher when the buzzer sounded. She froze like a deer trapped in the headlights of an oncoming car. *Her mother.* And everything wasn't nearly clean yet. She looked around at the tiny kitchen and then made a desperate decision. She would stack all of the dishes that could fit into the dishwasher and hide the rest. At some point in the middle of the night, when her mother was sound asleep, she would get up and, without her knowing it, wash the hidden ones.

She slammed the dishwasher closed with a leg, turned the knob on the front of it to the wash cycle, and then hustled about grabbing up the other things. The buzzer sounded again, and with her arms filled with crusty pots, she rushed across to the front door to bellow, "I'm coming! I'm coming!"

One of the heavy pots fell out of the pile and dropped on her toe at that point, and Marcel's shriek coincided with the entire lot in her hands clattering to the floor. She just barely managed to avoid the avalanche by doing some pretty fancy dancing on the spot. She massaged her toe with one hand while gathering up pots and other utensils with the other.

With the taxi driver's help, it would take her mother exactly three minutes to unload all of her luggage. She knew the way her mother usually operated. One bag first. A little one. Ring the bell. Go back for the rest. Marcel fully realized that she should be out there helping bring in the bags, but that couldn't be helped now. She had some clearing up to do.

Determination filled her. The world had been made in seven days. Let's see what she could accomplish in just three minutes.

She opened the cupboard beneath the sink and

began tossing everything in. Pots. Pans. Colanders. Knives. Forks. And a large flat pan, which still had the remnants of a piece of badly burnt shrimp stuck to it. She slammed the cupboard door shut at almost the very instant the knock sounded on the front door.

With her back against the sink, she wiped the flat of a palm across her forehead. *Thank the lord. She had done it.* She had actually done it. Her eyes swept the immediate surroundings. The house, at least on the surface of things, looked relatively respectable. She drew a filling breath. Yes, it was probably good enough to pass muster.

She ran her wet hands down the front of the robe, tightened the belt at her waist some more, and then shuffled across to the front door with a smile that was a little too wide pasted to her face. She snapped back the dead bolt, removed the chain, opened the door, and flung herself at the person standing on the threshold.

"I'm so glad you finally decided to come for a visit."

Chapter Twenty-Seven

Her body hit a solid wall of steel, and the impact was so very solid, and so very unexpected, that the shower cap covering her head was partially dislodged, and a thick swatch of hair escaped from one side of the plastic. Arms like twin bands of steel kept her from falling to the ground. She stared up at him through a curtain of haphazard hair, her mouth opening and closing without the benefit of any sound whatsoever. Then her eyes narrowed. What was he doing here? Come to finish off the deal, had he?

Ian maneuvered her back inside and closed and locked the door. The expression on his face was so concerned that Marcel almost broke out laughing. What an actor he was. But he couldn't get to her now. She knew what he was. Who he was.

"I left you a message telling you that I'd be coming by this morning." And he paused to give her another look. "Are you feeling all right? You look a little . . . strange. Did you get enough sleep last night?"

Marcel looked down at her horrible robe, her battered slippers, and then back up at him.

"I feel fine," she said coolly. "My, ah . . . my mother's coming to visit so I was just doing a little cleaning." Even though she intended to put him nicely in his place, now was just not the time. Besides, she wanted to choose when and how she would do it. She would go for his heart, the way he had tried to go for hers.

He smiled and despite everything, Marcel felt her heart do a crazy flip-flop in her chest. Lord, but he was good.

"That's really nice," he said warmly. "You know, I've never really heard you mention her before."

Marcel pushed the shower cap from her head and tried her level best to get her hair to lie flat against her skull.

"Well, my mother and I have a . . ." How would she put it? A difficult relationship? No. That wouldn't be right. "A complicated relationship."

Ian nodded. "I'm sure she just wants you to be happy."

Marcel made a noncommittal sound. He had no earthly idea of what he was talking about.

"You have brothers and sisters?"

"No. It's just me," Marcel said, and attempted to change the subject in a not-so-subtle manner. "I didn't get your message. Was it something important?" She hadn't listened to all her messages. The one from her mother had thrown her into a complete tizzy. "I would've dressed if I'd known you were coming."

"I just wanted to see you again." He stroked a hand down the side of Marcel's cheek before she could avoid him. "And I also wanted to invite you over to my house for dinner. Daniella's very curious about you. But now that your mother's here, I'd like to invite you both. Any night this week."

Marcel's mouth popped open. What? Invite her and her mother to dinner at his house? Was he out of his mind? Did he have any understanding at all of what that would do? It would be like waving red meat before a rabid dog. Her mother would decide instantly that she should marry Ian. Besides, Marcel didn't know if she could fake it that much, all the way, a dinner with his niece.

"No. We couldn't. We're going to be very . . . very busy this week. Besides—"

"OK. What about this weekend? Or maybe one day, say, next week? Better yet, you pick the date."

He had her, but before she could formulate the appropriate response, the doorbell rang again. Marcel's nostrils flared. It was definitely her mother this time. There was no question about it.

She quickly opened the front door. There was a pile of suitcases there, but no one to be seen. Marcel turned around with the beginnings of a frown between her eyes. Undoubtedly the working visit her mother was making could last a good long while.

"I'd better go out to help," she said. "She seems to have a lot of luggage. She's probably paying the driver."

"You stay," Ian said, and he placed a hand on her arm. "I'll get the rest of her things."

"No!" Marcel said frantically. "I think it might be best if you just snuck out the back door. You can wait until she's inside, then you can break into a run or something. That way you'll be able to get into your truck and go without her seeing you."

Ian's eyebrows lifted. "Break into a run? Are you sure you're feeling OK?"

Marcel gave him a sage look. "I'm feeling OK, but you won't be for too long if she gets a good look at you."

Ian threw back his head and laughed. "What're you talking about? I'd love to meet your mother. I want to meet the woman who gave birth to—"

But she cut him off with a wave of her hand. "Look, you may find this hard to believe because you've never met her, OK? But trust me on this one. She's . . . she's not easy to deal with."

Ian shoved his hands into his pockets and gave her a very tolerant look.

"And don't look at me like I'm crazy," Marcel said. "Do you have any interest in getting married?" She didn't wait for a response. "No. Of course you don't. So, as I was saying, you'd better go and go quickly before— Oh God . . . she's coming. Damn."

The stout woman coming up the gravel path nodded as if she was in total agreement with what had just been said.

"That's right, honey. Damn. Your mother is here. The same mother who suffered through sixty-four hours of the worst pain any human being has ever experienced. Just so she could bring you into the world. The same mother who had to risk her life flying three thousand miles across the country, then catch a taxi at an airport where no one speaks any English, travel for three more hours in a traffic jam on a parkway filled with crazy people, and then bring her own luggage up from the taxicab stopped on the road. Just so she can get a chance to see her only child. But . . ." and she shrugged in a manner that sent cold chills down Marcel's spine. ". . . that's just the kind of mother that I am. There isn't anything I wouldn't do for my daughter."

Marcel rushed out to grab at the bag in her mother's hand, smiling so hard that her face actually hurt. God in heaven, when was this day going to end? Better yet, how was it going to end? What could happen to her next? What?

"Mom," she said. "I'm sorry I couldn't come to pick you up. But you didn't even tell me you were coming . . . and you forgot to give enough information in the message you left on the answering machine."

Her mother pushed her aside. "Don't 'Mom' me." And she picked up a suitcase and struggled in with it.

"Please. Let me, Mrs. . . . ah, Templeton." Ian stepped over the half-dozen or so bags now neatly blocking the entrance to the house and picked up two of the largest ones.

"Oh, thank you," her mother said, and she appeared to really notice Ian for the first time. "What a very polite young man." Then she jabbed a not-so-polite elbow into Marcel's ribs and whispered, "So *this* is what you've been hiding from me."

Marcel swallowed. This was exactly what she'd been afraid of. Exactly what she had warned Ian against. She held on to her tongue with difficulty and bent to help with the other sundry bags and boxes. If only Ian had listened to her. But it was too late now. And he would soon see how very late it was.

"Where's the taxi driver, Mom?" Marcel asked as Ian grabbed the final bag and carted it in.

Her mother brushed the question off with a little wave of her hand. "Oh, I told him not to bother himself. If I managed on my own this far, I can certainly manage to carry the bags the rest of the way."

Marcel shot Ian a rapier glance. He was in the process of stroking a finger down the bridge of his nose, but she could tell that he was laughing at her. He thought the entire situation was deeply amusing. Well, once her mother started in on him, he'd be grinning all over the other side of his face. That much was certain.

"Mother . . . Mom . . . this is Ian Michaels."

Her mother straightened from whatever it was she was doing over one of the suitcases and enveloped Ian in a warm hug.

"So," she said, putting him away from her after the long moment of forced hugging. "You are the boyfriend she's been hiding?"

Ian's gaze darted to Marcel and then back to her mother. "Yes, ma'am," he agreed in a manner that made Marcel long to slap him solidly. He wasn't her boyfriend. They both knew that.

Mrs. Templeton stepped back with both hands now balanced on her ample hips. "So, how long has this been going on? You know my daughter can't wait around forever." She gave Marcel the kind of look that made fear run like liquid fire through her blood. "You know, Marcel's father and I decided within two weeks of going out together that we were going to get married. So," and she fixed Ian with a very direct stare, "is there something wrong with my daughter?"

Marcel put her hand over her eyes. *Here we go. This is it.*

"No, it isn't that at all. She's a beautiful—"

"So, why are you in her house, at this time of the day, with her dressed in that . . ." she waved a hand ". . . thing she's wearing? Are you saying that Marcel usually entertains you dressed like that?"

Ian's eyes shot to Marcel's face and she did nothing to hide the smirk she was feeling. *So, he wasn't so amused anymore, was he?*

But he tried again. Valiantly. "Well, I'm sure you have nothing to worry about there, Mrs. Templeton. Marcel is—"

"Worry?" Mrs. Templeton interrupted him with some amount of heat. "Don't tell me what to worry about. Let me ask you a question. . . ."

Marcel bent her head and prayed. *O Jesus, if I've ever done anything good in my life, please help me now. Don't let her say anything embarrassing. Please help her to keep her tongue in check. She's just trying to help. In her own way, she's just trying to help. I know that. But other people don't seem to understand.*

She had barely opened her eyes again before the words were out of her mother's mouth, "What's your name again, honey?"

"Ian, ma'am. Ian Michaels. And I think I'd better get go—"

"You can stay long enough to answer me this question, can't you?"

Ian smiled and agreed in a very pleasant voice that he could indeed stay for as long as she liked. But Marcel, sensing the coming disturbance, whispered in a fierce undertone, "Quick. Run, *run*."

But it was too late to even consider the possibility of suddenly sprinting unexplainably from the house. So Ian squared his shoulders and stood his ground.

"Tell me . . . Ian. What would you do if your thirty-year-old daughter couldn't find herself a husband? Any kind of husband?"

Beads of sweat broke out on Marcel's forehead in response to the softly spoken query, and she came to a quick decision. There was only one thing, one thing she could do. One thing alone that would put an end to the entire mess. It was drastic, yes. But she had no other choice. What she was about to do now was being done for the good of them all.

She drew a long pulling breath and then dropped to the floor like a stone.

Chapter Twenty-Eight

The sound Marcel made as she slumped to the floor was sufficiently loud to startle the entire room into complete silence. Ian was the first to react. In an instant, he was down on the floor.

"Marcel? My God. Are you hurt?" His fingers probed her neck for a pulse, and the deep concern in his voice caused Marcel to open an eye just a little.

"I'm OK," she hissed. "Save yourself. Go now!"

Ian looked up at Mrs. Templeton, who was standing frozen, with a hand pressed to her mouth.

"I think she's going to be OK," he said, and there was a flicker of humor dancing behind his eyes.

"OK?" Marcel's mother exclaimed. "She's practically half-dead. Look at her!" She pushed Ian aside. "She's going to go into convulsions and swallow her tongue any time now if we don't do something fast! She used to get these spells when she was a little girl, you know. Probably why she can't get herself a long-term man today. I mean, who would put up with this sort of thing? A man wants a healthy woman, not someone who'll drop into a dead coma over a pan of macaroni and cheese. Get me some wet rags."

"Mrs. Templeton, I really think she's—"

"Did you hear what I said?"

Ian nodded. "Yes, ma'am. Wet rags." He looked about the kitchen, his eyes hunting every available surface. *Wet rags. Wet rags. Now where in the name of heaven was he to find those?*

Mrs. Templeton gave him a look of exasperation. "Check by the sink. She always has rags somewhere there."

Marcel's eyelids fluttered in sudden panic. *No, no! He couldn't open up any of the drawers by the sink. What was happening? Was she cursed?*

She tried a very scratchy-sounding, "I'm OK, Mom," and attempted to rise. But her mother shoved her back down.

"Don't you move a muscle. You're sick, and Mama's here. Mama's right here, baby. Ian?" she yelled. "Get me those rags."

"I'm trying, Mrs. Templeton. I'm trying. But she doesn't seem to have any rags anywhere at all," Ian said, pulling open drawer after drawer in the little kitchen and hunting around unsuccessfully inside.

A little smile touched the corners of Marcel's mouth. Panic. It was panic that she heard in his voice. Very good. She had tried to warn him even though he had deserved no such consideration.

"Jesus, Mary, and Joseph," Mrs. Templeton said, heaving herself to her feet. "If you want anything done these days, you have to do it yourself. Come. Come, honey," she said to Ian, who was now in the process of ransacking one of the cupboards. "You keep her head elevated and let me find the rags. OK?" And she made a beeline for the sink, muttering heavily beneath her breath about the general uselessness of young people today.

"Stop her!" Marcel whispered as Ian knelt again beside her. "Don't let her open the—"

"Ssh," Ian said, and Marcel gave him a blistering look. "You're sick, honey. Don't talk. Your mother's getting some rags for you. Wet ones. You'll soon be all right."

"OK," Marcel whispered back in a fierce undertone. "OK. Fine. Go ahead. You think this is funny. You haven't seen anything yet, buddy. She's just getting started. I can predict what she'll—"

But the rest of what she had been about to say was suddenly disrupted by the solid crash of ten or so pots and other sundry items, tumbling from beneath the sink onto the kitchen floor. Mrs. Templeton's cry of, "Jesus, Lord!" brought Marcel up like a flash from her position on the ground.

She was on her feet in time to witness the heaviest pot of them all rolling from out of its hiding place beneath the sink. The large aluminum pot canted for a second on its side and then flopped over, spilling its contents out onto the floor and scattering burnt shrimp, pasta, corn, and other assorted vegetables in every conceivable direction.

Time seemed to come to a complete standstill for a moment, and Marcel watched in horrified fascination as a solitary green pea rolled all the way across the white kitchen tiles. She closed her eyes for a fraction as the pea settled somewhere deep beneath the refrigerator. Her hand went to grip Ian's arm as her mother looked silently down at the carnage and then back up at her.

The expression on her mother's face was one that Marcel was completely unfamiliar with, and she took a long slow breath and waited for the inevitable explosion. *This time, this time, she was really going to faint.*

Later, Marcel lay, curled into a little ball on her big four-poster bed with her eyes closed. He was making it so hard for her to hate him. Ian had suddenly taken charge. He had taken her by the arm and maneuvered her out of the hot zone and into the bedroom. Then he went back into the kitchen and Marcel could hear him saying in a soft, soothing manner, "It's going to be OK, Mrs. Templeton. It's going to be OK."

Then there was the murmur of her mother's voice saying something that Marcel couldn't quite make out. And Ian's voice saying again, "It's just a little food. You go and have a seat and let me take care of everything." And now the man was actually out in her kitchen washing her dirty dishes and talking to her mother in the most patient and tolerant manner.

She rolled onto the flat of her back and stared at the spackled white ceiling. Everything was just so confusing. This little thing with Ian had started out as just a bit of fun. Nothing serious. But she was beginning to feel something for him, despite her rules, despite what he had done, despite *everything*. And he, of course, probably thought that she was completely psychotic. The kind of person who would lose her own children at the supermarket. She was messed up. Her life was messed up. And, no matter what she did, what she tried, it would always turn out exactly like this. An utter and total catastrophe. And for him, she had just been a means to an end.

She sniffed piteously. She was going to do the adult thing and tell him that she had made a mistake. She didn't want the affair between them both to continue. There was no point to it. Not for him. Not for her. And she would also tell him that she knew who he was and that she wouldn't sell her magazine to him, not for any amount of money.

For the next little while, the sounds of pots banging, water running, and her mother's voice rising and falling over the entire racket made Marcel shut her eyes again and pray for a resolution to everything. She wiped a hand across her eyes and almost jumped out of her skin at the sound of a voice saying softly in her ear, "Everything's OK, my sweet. Don't cry."

Marcel's eyes sprang open to see Ian sitting on the bed beside her. She hadn't heard him come in. For a big man he moved very quietly.

She swallowed hard. "I'm not crying. Remember, I told you that I never cry."

He nodded. "I remember. But everyone cries, Marcy, and there's no shame in it."

Tears welled in Marcel's eyes. He really shouldn't speak to her as though he cared. It was cruel. Unnecessary.

"Don't play with me," she said in a strained voice. "I really can't take any more of it. All of you men . . . you hurt me so much. And . . . and I'm not as strong as I seem."

Ian sat on the corner of the bed and gathered her in his arms. "I'm sorry that other men have hurt you, Marcel. But is it fair to judge me because of what they've done?"

She sniffled against his chest. "I know about you," she said. She felt him stiffen.

"What about me?"

"You own the company that's trying to run me out of business."

She straightened away from him so that she could look him in the eye.

"You're Tyson Media."

He took a deep breath, his big chest rising and falling, and his face took on a pensive expression. "I was going to tell you. Just not right now."

Marcel blew her nose in a tissue. "Anyway," she said in a voice that was decidedly more sturdy now, "it doesn't matter. I understand everything, and it's OK."

He stared at her. "What do you understand and what's OK?"

"Well, there's no point to you . . . and me anymore. I'm not going to sell. Ever. I promised my dad."

"That had nothing to do with us. I didn't even know *Le Beau Monde* was your magazine until you told me about your dad."

"I don't care," Marcel said, and she came to her feet. "It was a mistake getting involved with you. So . . ." And for a moment the actual words failed her. "We should end this. Now. Before—"

He stood, too, and they stared at each other across the distance. "What if I told you that I didn't want your magazine anymore? Would you still want to end things between us?"

Marcel stared at him, wanting to cry, wanting to throw her arms around him. But she couldn't. She couldn't go down heartache road again. "No," she said, "I can't be the same fool twice . . . And you can never be the right one for me."

Ian continued to stare at her. He looked as if he wanted to grab her and shake her . . . or hold her and never let go. "Fine," he said. "Fine." And without another word, he turned and left the bedroom. Shortly afterward the sound of his truck starting in the driveway drew her to the window. With dry eyes she watched him go. It was for the best. It was.

Chapter Twenty-Nine

"Marcel? Come on, child, wake up."

Marcel rolled over in bed and threw a hand across her eyes. *Her mother.* It was her mother's voice. Had she answered the phone in her sleep? Maybe if she ignored it, the voice would go away.

She squeezed her eyes tightly shut and burrowed even deeper into the warm blankets. Sweet sleep drifted softly over her again, and slowly, she gave herself up to it. *She was so tired. So very tired . . .*

"Marcel? I know you hear me talking to you. Wake up."

This time, something hard and completely unforgiving prodded her in the ribs. She groaned and opened a sleep-reddened eye. There was someone standing right over her. She blinked and tried to focus. It *was* her mother. Marcel groaned. What did she want? Hadn't all of the talking last night been enough? Fortunately, there hadn't been a big scene after Ian left as she had greatly feared, but there had been a lot of talking about just about *every* subject under the sun. Hygiene. Men. Grandchildren. Time running out. Surely her mother had exhausted all of her most favorite subjects?

Marcel peered at the bedside clock and groaned again.

"Mom, it's only five o'clock in the morning. Why're you up so early? We only went to bed a few hours ago. Come on, go back to bed."

Mrs. Templeton sat on the edge of the bed. "Now's not the time for sleeping, honey. You can sleep all day long if you like, after."

Marcel threw her arm back over her eyes. "After? After what?"

Her mother stroked a hand over Marcel's wild hair. "When's the last time you went to the hairdresser? You know, men like a woman with nice-looking hair."

Marcel grunted something barely intelligible and prepared to ease herself back into sleep again. If her mother didn't want to sleep, that was fine, but she was certainly going to get some more shut-eye. She needed her strength. She still had to figure a way to save her magazine. She was not convinced at all that Ian had no interest in it any longer. The *San Diego Business* magazine had described it as a key part in

Tyson's West Coast strategy. So, why would Ian abandon that now? It didn't make any sense. He was well known for his ruthless business tactics.

She burrowed deeper beneath the blankets and reached as hard as she could for sleep. She had lost her hope for a second there last night. What with the fainting, the screaming, the pots falling every which way. Any normal mortal would've caved in to despair for a scant second during the confusion. But now she was better. She could see clearer now with the passing of the night. All was not lost. *But why was her mother still talking?*

"What'd you say?" Marcel croaked hoarsely.

"You know why I'm here, don't you, honey dear?"

Marcel cracked an eye open. "You said you'd come on a working visit or something like that."

The bed creaked beneath their combined weight.

"I was in my bed a few days ago . . ."

"Um-hmm," Marcel mumbled.

". . . I was reading my Bible and doing my affirmations. And, all of a sudden, just out of nowhere, something said to me, 'Marcel needs you. Go to Marcel.' "

Marcel rolled over and pulled up the blankets. "That's nice, Mom."

"Don't 'That's nice, Mom' me. This is important."

Marcel sat up, giving up on any hope for extra

sleep, and pushed back the thick tumble of hair from her eyes.

"OK, Mom. I'm listening. What're you trying to tell me? What's important?"

Her mother smiled and Marcel's heart fluttered with dread. She knew that look. And more often than not, it meant that her mother was about to reveal something that would bring along with it complete mayhem, havoc, pestilence, and destruction.

"I couldn't understand it at the time the Word came to me, but now I understand."

Marcel rested a hand against the blunt of her forehead. *Sweet Jesus.*

She swallowed. "Mom, please don't—"

"Shush, baby, and listen to me. I came here to help you get that man."

Marcel played dumb for a moment, hoping against hope that maybe by some miracle a tactic that had never worked in the past might just this once come through for her.

"What man, Mom? There's no man in my life right now. I told you that, remember? Ian . . . Ian was just joking last night when he said that he was my boyfriend. He's not."

Marcel was subjected to the kind of long and very direct stare that would've had lesser mortals trembling in their boots. Then, her mother went in for the kill.

"Is it me who wants you to get married? Am I

the one forcing you?" Yes, Marcel wanted to shout, but wisely kept her mouth shut. "Maybe you don't really want to." Her mother began pulling the blankets that had been cast aside back up over Marcel's legs. "Some women are like that. They prefer a quieter life. Children can be a handful." She laughed. "Who would know that better than me? Get some cats from the pet store, darling dear. Walk around all day dressed in your bathrobe if you prefer it. And when the time comes, if you manage to save enough money, you can just move right on into one of those nice retirement communities. You'll be able to sleep all day in your diapers then. And maybe at night you'll play bingo and shuffleboard. I've heard it's not such a bad life."

Her mother patted her on the leg and prepared to rise.

"You sleep, honey. You're tired. Too tired for all of this mess. Sleep. Sometimes it's better not to have a man. Maybe you can do better all by yourself . . . you and your pets."

Marcel pushed the blankets away. She was breathing as hard as if she had just run a 100-meter sprint. Why did she give in to it all the time? Why couldn't she ever just not listen to her?

"Ian doesn't want me, Mom. He only wanted the magazine . . . that's *all* he wanted."

"He only wants what? Are you blind, child? Did

you see how he just jumped right back in there last night and washed up all of your dirty, filthy dishes?" She patted Marcel's leg again. "That's a good sign honey. A good sign. It means he wants you. Not your dad's magazine. And," she continued, before Marcel could even get a word in, "he's good to look at, too. And polite." She drew breath and then charged on. "There aren't too many men around like that anymore, honey baby. And if you don't recognize that and go for him with everything you've got, some other woman will. And he's ready." She nodded. "Yes, he's ready to marry. It's there in his eyes. In the way he looks at you. Trust more than fifty years of experience on that."

Marcel pursed her lips. If Ian was ready for marriage, maybe somebody should tell him about it, because he sure as the devil didn't have a single solitary clue that he was.

"So? You have nothing to say? I come all this way to help you get this man—this *good-looking* man—and all you can do is just sit there and look at me?"

Marcel released a tight breath. "It's not as easy as you think, Mom. There's been some . . . things between us, and . . . well, to put it simply, I'm not too fond of him right now. Besides, he's not the right man for me."

Her mother laughed. "What's not to be fond of? And what do you mean, not the right man for you?

Is that why he was here in your house with you practically naked?"

"He had a reason," Marcel said stubbornly. "He came to pass on a message."

"The only message he had for you yesterday was 'Please let me in because I'm ready for a booty call.' "

Marcel's mouth dropped, and she stared at her mother in disbelief. Did her mother just say *booty call*?

"It was definitely not a *booty call*, Mom," she said, swinging her legs off the bed. "Like I said, he wants to buy the magazine. That's why he started dating me and that's as far as his interest in me goes."

"And, like I said, it's much more than just that, honey girl. And I don't know why you're hanging on to that business. I really blame your father for doing this to you. It was his dream, not yours. I know how much you loved him, and how seriously you take any promise you make, but really, child, you have to have a life, too."

Her mother got up, went across to the large four-poster bed, and began straightening the covers. "You see, what you don't know, what you don't understand, is," and she flapped a large white pillowcase and then dragged it over a goose down pillow, "that when it comes to settling down, most men usually don't know what it is they want or what's really best for them. Sure, you talk to them after twenty, thirty years of marriage and they'll tell you the whole thing was their idea. But," she gave Marcel a very direct look, "if you really want to get the *real* story, you talk to the women. The wives. They'll tell you what's up. They'll tell you that the only reason they're married today is because they took ahold of that man and didn't let go. That they caught him in the right way, so he would stay caught."

Marcel bit her lip. It was all she could do to prevent herself from breaking out into a big grin.

"Mom," she said, trying not to laugh, "have you been watching a lot of late-night TV lately?"

Her mother paused in her busy activities. "Oh, you think I don't know what I'm talking about, is that it? You think that I got this old by just knowing nothing at all?" She walked briskly to the other end of the bed and smoothed and folded the blankets neatly just below the pillow line. "If you want that man, Marcel, you'll listen to what I have to say."

Marcel went around and helped her pull the coverlet up over the blankets.

"All men are the same, honey. That's the first thing you have to understand about them. They're all the same. They all want basically the same things. They just come in different packages. Some tall, some short, black, white, and in between." She straightened. "But they're essentially the same man. Take your father, for instance."

Marcel's brow furrowed as she bent to tidy her bed. *Oh lord.* She didn't want to hear this. She had known for years before their actual divorce that her parents hadn't been getting along very well. It had actually been a huge relief when they split. It had brought an end to the constant fighting.

"You told me that Dad proposed to you after your sixth date."

Her mother walked into the bathroom and collected the mop and bucket that Marcel had stashed behind the door just the night before.

"I only told you that so you wouldn't think badly of him."

Marcel followed her out to the kitchen. "Mother, I did the kitchen floor yesterday. You really don't have to clean it again."

"Your kind of clean," she bent, opened the cupboard beneath the sink, and removed a large bottle of floor cleaner, "and my kind of clean are two totally different things. Just stay out of my way for a minute. Sit on one of those stools."

Marcel resigned herself and sat.

"What your father proposed, after our sixth date," she said, "was that we live together. I was young in the church then, and I could've done it. Why not? Your father was the kind of man who could've made you do almost anything he set his mind to.

"The thing is, when he asked me to move in with him, I wanted to, but I didn't. Why? Because I listened to what my mother had to say about it. In those days, children—no matter how old they were—used to listen to their parents. My mother sat me right down on the stoop and talked to me. She said, 'Annie, if you want to keep that boy around, don't make yourself cheap with him.' "

Marcel massaged her temples. "Mom, before you go any further. You have to believe me. Ian and I, well . . . we decided from the start that it would never work out between us. And I'd love to sit here and talk about this some more, but I've got to head over to Tracy's." She walked over and pecked her mother on the cheek. "We'll spend some time together later." *If I can bear it.*

Marcel turned and walked out of the room, missing the determined look in her mother's eyes.

In a little under an hour, Marcel pulled into Tracy's long curving driveway at breakneck speed, the car wheels kicking up small stones. She brought the car to a stop right next to Tracy's blue sports model. It was almost ten o'clock, and her husband, Tommy, was away for the weekend, so she knew Tracy had to be awake. And if she wasn't, it was high time she got her lazy behind out of bed.

Marcel climbed from the car, armed the alarm, and then walked up the short flight of stone stairs that led to the white front doors, and rang the doorbell.

After a good stretch there was the sound of soft footsteps, and then the door opened.

"God," Tracy said, lifting a hand to shield her eyes from the early-morning sunshine. "What time is it?"

Marcel stepped into the cream faux marble foyer. "Girl," she said. "Don't tell me you're still in bed. Are you sick?"

Tracy shut the door. "Not sick. Just tired. I didn't get to bed until after twelve—"

Marcel didn't give her a chance to continue. "My whole life's falling apart," she said, putting a hand to her face. "Everything's a mess."

Tracy reached out to squeeze her arm. "Whatever it is, we'll fix it. Come in and tell me all about it."

Chapter Thirty

Ian pulled into Marcel's driveway, cut the engine, and hopped from the truck almost in one fluid motion. He'd been trying to get ahold of Marcel for the better part of the morning. He had spent a good long time last night thinking about their parting conversation and it had occurred to him that this entire misunderstanding could have been avoided had he just been completely honest with her from the very beginning. Now he had to undo the damage. Fast. Because without him even realizing when or how it had happened, he had developed feelings for her. Strange, deep feelings. And he wouldn't let anything come between them. Not anything. He couldn't get her out of his mind. She had gotten under his skin. Last night, for the first time ever, he had found himself unable to work. He had played with Daniella until it was time for her to go to bed, and then, as was his usual practice, he had gone to sit out on the veranda to take care of the day's business. But he had found himself jumpy and irritable. The ocean, a body of water that he had always had a great deal of love for, bothered him. It was too loud. Too restless. And he had gotten out of his chair to pace back and forth on the large wraparound deck. But nothing had seemed to calm him. He had tried one of Vera's hot chocolate and rum concoctions. But the sweet warmth of that had brought back memories of the heat of Marcel's thighs, the curl of her lips, the soft texture of her velvet tongue.

It was no good. He had to have Marcel with him.

Ian jingled the keys in his pocket and rang the doorbell. He waited a few seconds only and then lifted a hand to hammer on the wooden door. She was obviously hiding from him and there was no way he was going to let her.

He was just in the process of knocking on the door again when, to his complete surprise, it was suddenly yanked open.

"Well, it's about time." And Mrs. Templeton, without any hesitation, grabbed him by the hand and pulled him into the house.

Ian very nearly tripped over a bucket and mop standing right inside the doorway.

"Just push that bucket aside, honey," Mrs. Templeton said. "Marcel's not back yet. But I'm glad you came over. It'll give us some time to have a nice visit."

Ian smiled at her and bent to retrieve the bucket and mop.

"Actually, Mrs. Templeton," Ian said, once the metal pail was out of the way, "I came by to have a talk with Marcel." He cleared his throat. "We had a little disagreement yesterday. And—"

"Um-hmm," Mrs. Templeton said, then turned and walked into the dining room. Ian followed and saw her laying down place mats. "Ian, honey," she said, "hand me some knives and forks. They're in the drawer just beneath the sink there. No, the one on the right."

Ian pulled the drawer open and extracted a pair of nicely matched ivory-handled forks.

"Two?" he asked, holding them up for her to see.

"And two knives."

Mrs. Templeton beamed a smile of approval as he walked around the mini-bar area to hand her the utensils.

"Get me some glasses now, dear. You'll find them in the cupboard just above the bar."

Ian got the glasses and handed them over. He was actually beginning to feel quite pleased that Marcel was not at home. It would give him some time to talk to her mother. To really understand what he had to do in order to break down Marcel's resistance to him.

He helped put the final touches on the table and then settled into a chair with fingers steepled beneath his chin.

When Mrs. Templeton was satisfied that the table had been set to her satisfaction, she turned to Ian with a diamond-bright gleam in her eyes.

"You know, honey," she began, "I can see that you're a good man."

Ian thanked her, but Mrs. Templeton waved a hand at him to indicate that she was not yet through with her thought.

"Yes, you're a good man. But you know, dear heart, there are things that you can do to correct your little problem."

Chapter Thirty-One

"Mom? I'm home!" Marcel dropped her purse on the kitchen counter at almost the very moment that her mother came bustling out of the bedroom.

"You're finally back, dear heart. Come, zip me up," and she turned to present Marcel with the open back of her dress. "Hurry, love. Hurry. I think the chicken's burning."

"Did anyone call?" She waited countless seconds. And in the moments of waiting she prayed that Ian had ignored everything she had said to him earlier and had called anyway.

"Oh, yes," her mother said, and walked across to the stove to lift a pot cover. She prodded a piece of chicken with the tip of a cooking fork and nodded in satisfaction when no pink flesh appeared.

"And . . . ? Who called? Did you answer, or did you let the machine get it?"

"Oh, I didn't have time for the phone, dear, I was too busy talking to your Ian."

Marcel's heart stopped beating for a fraction of a second. Oh lord. She had not thought for even one second that he might actually stop by. There was no telling what her mother must have said to him. No telling at all.

"Did he say anything?"

Mrs. Templeton turned. "Hand me that dish."

Marcel handed over the large transparent Pyrex dish. "Mom? Did he say anything? Why he came by, I mean?"

Her mother plunged the fork into the bubbling oil and lifted out a perfectly crusted golden thigh.

"For someone who isn't interested in this man, you sound pretty anxious."

Marcel smoothed the damp away from her palms against the front of her dress. She had to be calm. She just had to be.

"So, he left a message for me then?"

Another perfectly fried golden leg was placed in the bowl, and then her mother wiped her hands on a damp cloth.

"We had a good long talk. And I cleared up a lot of things with him."

"Things?" Marcel croaked. "What things?"

She smiled suddenly, and Marcel's heart fluttered as cold fear coursed through her veins.

"You didn't say anything . . . anything funny, did you, Mom?"

Her mother shot her a gleaming little look. "Funny? Funny? What am I, a comedienne? We had a nice long talk. A nice long talk. I asked him questions. He gave me answers. He's a nice, polite young man. And," she said, turning to her pot again, "I told him that I'd be happy to have him as a son-in-law."

Marcel stared at her mother in disbelief. "Mom, you didn't!"

Mrs. Templeton turned back toward the stove and busied herself over the bubbling oil. "A mother can dream, can't she? I didn't say that *you* wanted to marry *him*. As a matter of fact, I told him that you were out today . . . all day with Alex."

Marcel covered her mouth with a hand and repeated in a horrified manner, "Alex? Who's Alex?" Her mind was suddenly an utter and total blank. She had a horrible feeling that her mother had several other bombs in store for her. But somehow, for some reason, she was exercising a smidgen of pity and was letting them fall slowly, one by one.

Her mother shot her a rapier glance. "What do you mean, 'Who's Alex?' Isn't he the last man you thought you were going to marry? The one you couldn't stop talking about? The same one you then threw naked into the streets, no less than," she retrieved another piece of chicken, "two months after I started putting together your wedding guest list?"

"Oh God," Marcel groaned.

"I told him just what he needed to know, honey baby. And nothing else. I know you think my mind is going, Marcel child, but let me tell you, I'm not nearly senile yet."

"But you told him I was out with *Alex*."

Her mother nodded. "It's never a good thing to have a man think that he's the only horse in the race."

Marcel closed her eyes for a moment and massaged the pounding at her temples. "I'm going to lie down," she said, and she got slowly to her feet. There was no point in saying anything more. Her mother had a particularly extraordinary way of twisting situations, and she would twist and twist until things were so confused and so messed up that she actually started to make some form of sense.

"He wants you to come to dinner."

Marcel gripped the edge of the counter. Her heart had begun to thump heavily in her chest.

"He wants me to what?"

"Dinner. Tomorrow. At his house," her mother said. And she gave Marcel a brilliant smile. "He's going to call again later."

Without answering, Marcel turned and walked out of the kitchen, muttering beneath her breath. This was exactly what she'd been afraid of. Her mother just could not control her tongue. She stalked into the bedroom, yanked open the closet door, and cast a malevolent glare at the lump of clothes that she had hurriedly tossed on the floor just the day before. She would fold them all after her shower, she decided. Then she would decide if she was even going to accept Ian Michaels's invitation to dinner.

Chapter Thirty-Two

The next day, Marcel sat to put the finishing touches on her makeup. Outside, a blustery wind played with a cluster of dwarf coconut palms, tossing the nicely manicured heads back and forth and pulling the occasional strand of green from where it languished, and carrying it on a rollicking tumble across the narrow street. She had decided to have dinner with Ian after all. She had thought about things carefully, and had figured that she would go and see what he was up to now.

"Mom?" Marcel called out. "Are you sure he said eight o'clock?"

Her mother appeared in the doorway. "If you had been awake last night when he called, you would know yourself what time he said."

Marcel sucked in a little breath. *Calm. Today she had to be absolutely calm.*

Marcel gave herself a moment and filled in the brief silence by stroking a dark kohl eyeliner beneath her eyes. When she was completely sure that nothing could possibly disturb her, she said very nicely, "I tried calling him back last night after I woke up, but he didn't answer."

"And you didn't think to call him today? Did you leave him a message last night?"

Marcel fitted the lipstick back together and stood. "I left him a message. And I didn't call him back today because he didn't return my call."

"Playing hard to get," her mother said, shaking her head, "will not get you that man, honey child. It might help you get yourself some *other* man, but not that one."

"I'm *not* playing hard to get," Marcel snapped, then took a deep breath. If the truth be known, where Ian Michaels was concerned, she was probably still very easy to get. Extremely easy to get. And that was the problem, wasn't it? Despite the fact that all he had wanted was her magazine. She paused, remembering how intense, how focused, he had been when he'd gotten her into bed. She shivered. Well, maybe that hadn't been *all* he had wanted. And when she thought about how she had surrendered to him . . . No, he wasn't the right man for her, but she could enjoy him for a little while longer, until she had to make herself let him go.

"Well, at least this dress you're thinking of wearing should make up for your rude behavior."

Marcel ignored the "rude behavior" comment and said, "It is a nice dress, isn't it?" She got up and walked across the room to lift the beautifully spun creation from where it lay on the bed. She held it up to the light. It was simply one of the most gorgeous dresses she had ever seen. Wispy black. Stretchy. A tantalizing cobweb of silken thread that revealed almost as much as it concealed. And because the fabric was not a stiff one, the wonderful dips and swirls built into the design clung to her every curve in the most pleasing way. She imagined the look on Ian's face when he saw her in the dress, and shivered. She shouldn't be thinking this way. What was the matter with her? She wasn't supposed to even like him anymore. But she did. God, she did! And somehow, she just couldn't help it.

She slipped out of her robe and started to get dressed.

"You'd better hurry and finish dressing then. You know how you're always late for everything."

After she stepped into her black strappy high heels, she smoothed both hands down the front of the dress, then walked over to her full-length mirror to view the effect. She turned this way and that, then smiled. She looked good.

She spent a moment more before the mirror, bothering herself with little things. A final comb through her hair. The hot comb again, just to make sure that the areas just above her temples were silky straight. Then she stepped back and, satisfied, picked up her black velvet clutch purse, and walked out of her bedroom.

Her mother was standing over the stove when she entered the little kitchen.

"Mom," she said. "I'm ready."

Her mother turned and smiled at the picture she made. "You look beautiful, honey."

"You still taking the chicken? Men like good Southern fried chicken. And you know no one cooks a better bird than me."

Marcel smiled. "Thanks, Mom."

She turned back to the stove. "I've put everything in this nice white china bowl. It shouldn't be too hot for you to carry. And it should keep the chicken nice and crispy. I'm going to put a thin piece of paper toweling over the top. Remember to take it off as soon as you get there. And you'll tell him that you fried this chicken yourself. OK? Don't worry too much about being completely honest. It's never a good thing to be so completely honest with men.

"I'll just wipe the bottom off, so you don't get any grease on your dress. Are you going to be able to walk in those shoes? You know you have weak ankles."

Marcel shook her head. "Thanks for the chicken, Mom," she said, taking the dish from her. "Don't wait up."

"What do you mean, don't wait up?" her mother asked, eyebrows raised.

Marcel kept walking.

"Now don't give yourself away, Marcel Templeton," her mother said, hurrying after her. "If you do, he'll take what you give him, but he won't give you what you want."

"Don't worry, Mom," Marcel said, walking to her car. "I know how to handle Ian Michaels." She opened the passenger door and placed the dish of chicken carefully on the floor, closed the door, and walked over to the driver's side. She gave her mother a jaunty little wave before she slipped behind the wheel, and tooted the horn for good measure before she drove off.

Chapter Thirty-Three

Ian tied a lopsided bow to the base of Dani's fat braid and then turned her toward the mirror.

"Well?" he asked after a moment when she said absolutely nothing at all.

She turned back to him with the beginnings of a temper in her eyes. "It's not right," she said.

Ian rubbed a hand across his forehead and sat on the edge of the pretty pink-and-roses bed. "Dani," he said with great patience, "this is at least the fiftieth time we've done that bow. So, either you stay with it exactly as it is now, or you let Vera do it for you."

Her lower lip trembled. "No, I want you to do it."

Ian pinched the tip of his nose and tried to think of the best approach to take with her.

"Uncle loves you, and would do just about anything for you. But I just can't tie ribbons and bows the way you like." He took her by the shoulders. "You look very pretty and I dare anyone not to think so," he added solemnly.

"OK," Dani said just as solemnly.

"Good." Ian smiled. "Now, let's go out onto the back deck and watch for her car. Whoever sees the car first wins. OK?"

And she trailed after him in her frilly peach dress. They stopped by the large kitchen on the way out, and Ian went over to press a kiss to Vera's floured cheek.

"Everything going OK? You sure you can handle everything? You should really have let me hire some people to help you. I don't want you wearing yourself out."

The housekeeper shoved him away with a fond hand. "Go on with you," she said. "I'm not old and useless yet." She gave him a slap on the hand as Ian attempted to get a taste from her pan of corn bread. "Out," she said, pointing a finger at the door. "And I don't want to see you again until that young lady gets here."

And, with that affectionate admonishment, Ian walked out to the deck that faced the long twisting drive, placed Daniella neatly in one of the chairs, and then settled in himself to wait.

Marcel, just a half a mile away, marveled at the sheer size and beauty of the houses as she drove along the coast road. They were nothing less than mansions. And they all sat right on the very lip of the beach. Lord, but they were beautiful.

She drove on, turning her head every now and again to look at the beauty of the foaming ocean. It was so peaceful. So wonderful. But where was his house, for goodness' sake?

Then out of the golden twilight with its soft coral pink driveway, she saw it. And it was enormous. The largest house on the entire road. She took a deep breath and started up the long, winding driveway.

She parked right next to Ian's white truck and got out of the car, her heart pounding. She walked around to the other side and got the bowl of chicken from the passenger side and looked up at the house. She turned when she heard footsteps on the wooden stairs.

"I saw her first, Uncle! I saw her first!"

And then the familiar husky voice, "So, you came after all."

Tension trembled like a wild thing in the pit of Marcel's stomach as she froze for half a second. It was silly to be this nervous.

"I brought chicken," she said, coming forward now.

He came all the way down the stairs and gave her a swift kiss on the cheek. Marcel's heart did a dance in her chest at the feel of his lips on her skin. Then she looked down into a small pixyish face dominated by large velvet brown eyes.

She smiled. "And who are you?"

The little girl looked up at her with bald curiosity. "Dani," she said in a very bold manner, and Marcel had the distinct impression that she was being subjected to a very thorough inspection.

"That's a very pretty name."

She nodded. "Uncle named me. Not my daddy."

Marcel looked at Ian, and at the soft expression on his face, and felt a great warmth spread slowly through her heart.

"Well, come on up," he said and Marcel barely kept herself from trembling when he wrapped a strong arm about her. "I've got a surprise for you."

She sucked in a breath. "You do?"

"I do. But first, come meet Vera."

And together they walked up the stairs and into a huge sunken living room. Almost as soon as they entered, a short, plump woman with her head wrapped in a traditional Kente turban appeared.

"So, you're the young lady Ian can't stop talking about." Then she enveloped Marcel in a warm hug and pressed a kiss to the side of her face.

Marcel looked at Ian, surprised. He had spent time talking about her?

"Nice to meet you, too," she said with a slightly bemused note in her voice.

"Vera takes care of me, Dani, and everything else around here," Ian said, smiling. "I don't know what I'd do without her."

The old lady gave Ian a happy look and said with affectionate irritation in her voice, "You wouldn't do anything more than get yourself married. That's all. You certainly don't need me."

Ian patted the old woman's cheek and assured her that no matter what happened, he would always need her.

Marcel watched the interplay between the two, and a dawning realization came over her. This was his housekeeper, but he loved her. And she loved him right back. How strange. How wonderful. How absolutely the way things should be. He was sweet, decent, kind and, oh lord, she was beginning to have some deeply troubling feelings for him. How *was* she going to let this man go?

"I brought some chicken," she said, thrusting the china bowl at Vera.

Vera accepted it, then shooed them out onto the veranda.

"Go and sit," she said. "Dinner'll be ready in just a little while."

The rest of the evening proceeded without a hitch. They all sat around a long deck table and plunged into a long and very boisterous game of Monopoly.

One that Ian cheated mercilessly at. Marcel, at some point in the game, lifted Daniella to sit in her lap and said, "OK, Dani. Uncle's cheating, so we're going to put our heads together and beat him. OK?"

Shrieks of laughter flavored the salty ocean wind until Vera served dinner. Thick slabs of sweet corn bread, smothered steak with thick brown gravy, macaroni and cheese, Marcel's mother's crunchy chicken. And everything topped off with hearty slices of warm pumpkin pie and generous scoops of vanilla ice cream.

Ian put Daniella to bed at ten o'clock and Marcel couldn't help but stand and watch as he read her a bedtime story in the sweet intimacy of Dani's darkened bedroom. Marcel looked at him with soft eyes and a sudden realization came over her. This was what life was truly about. This caring. This dedication to family. This love. And she admitted silently to herself that she had never been this happy. Ever.

Later, they took a long walk along the beach and Marcel felt so carefree that she removed both her stockings and heels and walked barefoot in the sand.

Ian stopped her after they had walked a good stretch up the shore, and with the moon sitting like a giant watchdog just above his shoulder, took her face in his hands and asked, "Will you forgive a stupid man?"

Marcel blinked. He was actually asking her for

forgiveness? Her heart shuddered in her chest as sudden realization came over her. Lord Almighty. Did she love him? Had she gone and fallen in love with this man . . . this man she could not have—should not have?

Later, Marcel left Ian's house in such a haze of excitement that she drove all the way to Tracy's house and banged on the door until she was let in.

She stood in the living room now, trying to get ahold of herself.

"Take a deep breath and tell me again," Tracy said.

"He asked me to go away with him to Jamaica . . . a cruise," Marcel said after taking a gulp of air. "But I can't go—"

"Why can't you go?" Tracy asked in a patient manner.

"Because I . . . I love him. And he still wants that same no-strings affair." She covered her mouth with her hand. "Oh, God, why did I agree to this? Was I out of my mind?"

"Listen," Tracy said, and she fixed Marcel with a steady, no-nonsense look. "You are going on this cruise, OK?" She held up a finger when Marcel drew breath to interrupt. "Yes, you are. And I don't want to hear any nonsense about your rules or anything you might have to say about it. You're going."

"But he doesn't love me."

"Please, girl, what man would go to all this trouble if his feelings weren't involved? What's the matter with you? Are you stuck on stupid?"

Marcel smiled despite herself. "OK, fine, I'll go on the cruise, but if things don't work out . . ."

"Everything will work out," Tracy said. She crossed to her friend and gave Marcel a hug. "Trust me, girl, things will work out."

Chapter Thirty-Four

Two weeks later Marcel stood in her bedroom going over her checklist of things she absolutely had to take along with her. It was only a seven-day cruise to Jamaica, but she would still need certain essentials. She picked up the slip of white paper again and stared at it. *Shoes. Three dressy dresses. Jeans. Lingerie from Tracy. Shorts. Bikini. Flip-flops. Underwear. Toiletries.* She wouldn't take the man-catching book, *The Technique*, in her bags, in case Ian found it. She would just have to call Tracy and ask her to read certain parts to her on the phone. Tracy might feel that Ian had a soft spot for her, but she wasn't at all sure that his feelings ran as deep as she wanted them to. She could just imagine him as her husband though. *Her husband.*

Marcel turned as her mother walked into the bed-

room. Nothing at all had been said about the im-
pending trip and Marcel eyed her warily now. "I'm
not committing a crime or anything, Mom. There's
no need to look like that."

Her mother walked across to the closet, opened
the door, and began taking out her clothes. Marcel
watched her without comment for a few seconds,
and then she went over and began replacing the
clothing on hangers. "What're you doing, girl?" It
was the first real bit of conversation that had passed
between them since Marcel's return from Ian's
house.

"You're not leaving," Marcel said now. "Not like
this."

"Why should I stay?" her mother shot back. "My
daughter's about to shack up with a man who isn't
her husband. She doesn't listen to a word I have to
say about it. She might even now be pregnant. I
wanted better than that for you. Much better. And I
won't stay here and watch you make a mess of your
life."

Marcel drew a steadying breath. She had known
this was coming. Had known it as surely as she knew
that summer followed spring. Why in the name of
heaven couldn't her mother just be happy for her?
Why did she always have to make such a federal
case out of everything? Did she even begin to understand how unhappy she had been in the last year?
How desperate? How panicked? All of the things,

the crazy mixed-up things she had done, like coming up with rules, had been done out of fear. And because of her incessant prodding and hinting about getting old and not having a man to depend on. God. Why did she do it?

"Mother," she said with a note of great patience in her voice. "Will you sit down for a moment?" Maybe if she spoke to her woman-to-woman, she would understand things better. Part of the problem between them had always been her mother's inability to recognize the fact that she was no longer a child. That she would never be a child again.

"I've got packing to do," her mother said without pausing in dragging sundry items from where they lay on the shelf above the hangers.

"Mom, please. Listen to me. *Listen to me.*" Her voice lifted so sharply that her mother actually paused in what she was doing and half-turned toward her.

"Are you raising your voice to me?" she asked, and there was a thick layer of ice in her voice.

"I am *not* a child anymore, Mother," Marcel said, and she did her best to control the volume and tone of her voice. "Can you understand that? I am not a child. Many women my age . . . Most women my age are married with their own families. When you were my age, you already had me. Doesn't that tell you anything? You were having sex with Daddy. You must have been or I wouldn't be here today."

Her mother turned toward her. "I wanted better than that for you. Better. Do you hear me? I raised you well. I raised you to stand on your own two feet. Not to . . . to go off and live with some man who doesn't respect you enough to make a decent woman of you."

"I am not going off to live with him, Mom. It's just a cruise. Just a little seven-day cruise."

Her mother gave a disdainful sniff and returned to folding her clothes. "I came down here to help you get yourself settled. But I can see now that it was a bad idea. I don't know you anymore. And you don't need me anymore. So there's no reason for me to stay any longer. I'll just get out of your way so you can carry on with your life . . . whatever way you like." And she began removing the suitcases she had arrived with.

Marcel walked into the bathroom and slammed the door. Her mother had been doing this to her all of her adult life. She knew exactly which buttons to press to get Marcel jumping through hoops. *But not this time. Not* this *time.* She was going to Jamaica with Ian, *and* she was going to have a *good* time, too. She might even get smashed if the mood took her.

She closed the toilet lid and plunked herself down on it. If her mother wanted to leave, then she would do nothing else to stop her. She was tired of the whole thing. Tired of trying to understand her. Tired of never getting through to her. Tired of having to behave like a child whenever she was around. This was where she drew the proverbial line in the sand and said *No more*.

Ian was coming to get her in two hours, and she would be ready to leave with him. And no matter what her mother said or did between now and then, she would not relent. Would not suddenly decide not to go just because "decent young unmarried women do not go off on cruises with unmarried men." This was the twenty-first century, for goodness' sake, and practically every so-called *decent* woman she knew of had gone off somewhere at some time with a man she was not married to.

She pulled a handkerchief from the pocket of her jeans, and dabbed furiously at the corners of her eyes. She wasn't going to start crying either. Her mother was probably just bluffing anyway. She always played a major scene whenever she didn't have things exactly the way she wanted them. But she wouldn't manipulate Marcel this time.

The phone sitting in the bracket on the wall began to ring and Marcel wiped her nose and got up to answer it. "Hello," she said in a watery voice.

"Hello yourself. Are you ready?"

Marcel sniffed, and then gave a very watery: "Almost."

Ian's playful tone changed immediately. "What's wrong? What's happened?"

She sniffed again. "It's. . . . it's nothing."

"Come on, Marcy. Don't you trust me yet? You can tell me. Whatever it is. What's the matter, you don't want to go anymore? You don't want to go and you don't know how to tell me? Come on. You've seen me naked."

"Don't say that too loudly," Marcel said in a very wintry voice. "My mother might hear you. And God knows that's all I need right now."

There was a brief silence, and then he said, "She doesn't agree with us going off together?"

Marcel wiped her eyes again. "My mother's very old-fashioned. And stubborn."

"I know someone who takes after her then," he teased.

Marcel sniffled and said, "Don't make me laugh. She's out there right now, packing."

"She's coming with us?"

"What?" Marcel exclaimed. "*No*. God forbid. She says she's going back home to New York."

Ian made a little sound of concern. "Maybe if I talked to her. She likes me, you know. We had a very long talk a while ago. She told me a lot of things about you."

Marcel blinked. "I know. What did she tell you though?"

The smile radiated in Ian's voice. "Nothing for you to worry yourself about. Just some things that I was confused about. Some things that I definitely needed to know."

Marcel groaned. She could just imagine what had been divulged. The thought of it made her cringe inside. Ian's voice rumbled in her ear, and Marcel dragged her mind back to the subject at hand.

"I'll explain that we'll have two separate cabins," he was saying.

Marcel's eyebrows lifted. *They would?* Naturally, she had assumed that they would both be staying in the same state room.

"We're not in the same room then?" And the disappointment in her voice was unmistakable.

Ian's voice deepened. "We are, unless you don't think it a good idea?"

"Oh no, no. It's fine. It's just that you just said that . . ."

"I thought of telling your mother that. You know. Just to reassure her that I'm not taking advantage of you."

Marcel gave a full-bodied chuckle this time. There was only one other person on earth who could make her laugh like this when she was feeling down. Tracy.

"No. I really don't think that'd do any good. She'd just think that I put you up to it."

"We should cancel then." And there was a faintly questioning note in his voice.

Marcel stood with more determination now.

"Don't you dare, Ian Michaels. My mother has to understand that she can't run my life anymore. She has to accept that I'm a grown woman capable of making my own decisions and living with the consequences. Just as she did herself."

Ian cleared his throat. "OK. But I want you to talk to your mother again. Tell her that I won't lay a single finger on you the entire trip. That I promise not to . . ."

"You'd better lay all of your fingers and toes on me during this trip," Marcel said in a decidedly more sturdy manner. "And you don't have to promise anything. But, I'll try talking to her again." Though it would do absolutely no good. She was dead sure of it now.

"I'll pick you up in an hour and a half or so then?"

Marcel nodded. "OK. I'll be ready. Drive carefully."

She hung up with a pensive expression in her eyes. Here she was standing right on the threshold of something she had wanted very, very much for the longest while, and instead of being happy that she was at least getting a little taste of what she wanted, she was absolutely miserable. She would go and talk to her mother again though. She would try one more time.

She opened the bathroom door and looked out. There were suitcases everywhere, but her mother was nowhere to be seen. Marcel walked across to the bed and began zipping together the two bags she was taking. It took her less than a minute to do this, and when she was through, she stood looking down at the two neat little shoulder bags. If she'd forgotten anything, it was just too bad. She'd have to buy it on board the ship.

With that taken care of, she went in search of her mother.

"Mom? Mother?"

She was standing by one of the windows in the sitting room, looking out. Marcel took a breath and then went to stand beside her.

"Mom, please stay until I get back. Please stay until at least then?"

Her mother said nothing for a moment, then she surprised Marcel with: "So you're all grown now?"

Marcel put a gentle hand on her arm and coaxed. "Don't worry, Mom. Remember you told me yourself how much you liked Ian? Remember that?"

Her mother sighed. "The cruise should come after the wedding. Not before. And I always wanted to be the one to give it to you. As a gift, you know? Now what will I give when you get married?"

Marcel wrapped an arm about her mother's waist, and they stood there in silence for several minutes, just breathing and watching the cars go by on the road below. She was so sorry that things hadn't worked out in the manner her mother would have liked. The big white wedding. The gathering of

friends and family. The food. The music. The joy
that finally, she, Marcel Templeton, the final unmarried woman in the world, was getting married. But,
that was reality. That was life. And at least she'd be
getting half of the deal. She'd have Ian at least for
a little while. Then . . . Well, she would deal with
"then" later.

Her mother looked up at her after a long moment.
"I'll only stay if you want me to stay. I don't want
to be in the way."

The words caught in Marcel's throat. *What?* Her
mother giving in? It couldn't be. It really, really
couldn't be. "You know I want you to stay. What
would I do without you?"

Chapter Thirty-Five

Marcel stood on a large spacious balcony looking down at the wide stretch of crystal blue sea. It was gorgeous, glorious, wonderful. She was really here with Ian.

She heard the door to their cabin open, so she turned and went back inside.

"There you are," she beamed at him. "I was wondering where you'd gotten to."

"Did you miss me?" he asked, and there was that deliciously playful note in his voice. His eyes met hers from across the distance and Marcel felt a thrill run through her. *Lord, but he was a gorgeous man. Inside and out.* And, at least for the next several days, he was going to be all hers. God certainly moved in very mysterious ways.

She went to Ian and wrapped long arms about his

middle. "Thank you for inviting me on this trip. Do you know I've never been to Jamaica before?"

He laughed, and tickled the tip of her nose. "Well, that's definitely something you'll never be able to say again." A pensive expression came and went in his eyes, and Marcel tightened her arms about him.

"What?"

He stroked the ridge running down the center of her back with slow deliberation. "I feel like having something to eat. Are you hungry?"

"Not for food," and she gave him a saucy little look.

He bent his head to kiss her. "Your mother . . . I don't want her to think any less of you because of this."

Marcel shushed him with a little sound. "She's fine. We had a nice long talk before you came to get me. And she . . . she understands."

He didn't seem convinced and Marcel laughed. "Sometimes I really don't know what she thinks about me."

Ian shifted her away so that he could look directly at her. His eyes were serious. "She loves you very much. She just has a different way of showing it. Now," and he pulled her in a bit closer, "I think what you need is some warm food in your stomach. Everything always seems a lot brighter after a good hearty meal." And before she could say anything to the contrary, he was already picking up the phone and dialing.

Marcel went across to sit on the bed. What was this sudden obsession with eating? Was he suffering from an attack of nerves? She pressed a hand to the flat of her stomach. Well, she would eat a little just to satisfy him, and then she would coax him very gently into bed. He wouldn't be nervous at all by the time she was through with him. She smiled at him as he hung up. "What'd you get?"

"I ordered from their . . . ah, special menu, so it'll be here in less than five minutes." He went across to draw the thick drapery and then spent a minute fiddling with the flowers in one of the fluted vases next to the window.

Marcel nodded to herself. He *was* nervous. But what had brought this on, for goodness' sake?

"Ian, sweetheart . . ." And she tried to think of how exactly to calm him. But he held up a finger at the knock on the door, and said, "Don't move a muscle. I'll be right back."

Marcel watched him with puzzled eyes as he walked across to pull open the door, and her jaw went slack with disbelief as a crowd of people entered the suite. For an instant, a jumble of emotions swarmed her. What in the world was going on? What were they all doing here?

Her gaze went to her mother first and then to Tracy and the half a dozen other people who had just entered. Her eyes dipped to the blood-red roses they each held, and Marcel stammered something barely intelligible.

"What's . . . ? What's going on? How . . . why're you all here?"

And then her bemused eyes went to Ian. He was going down on one knee. Oh Lord. She covered her mouth with a hand, and hot tears gathered behind her eyes. The crowd in the room faded away and above the faint buzzing in her ears, she heard him ask, "Marcel Anna Templeton . . . will you be my wife?"

Suddenly both her mother and Tracy were at her side, supporting her, and Marcel managed a strangled, "Yes, yes, yes!" And the most beautiful solitaire diamond ring was being placed on her finger.

Marcel turned swimming eyes to Tracy, who was beaming at her. She didn't understand any of it. But there would be time enough to sort everything out. Ian wrapped her in warm arms as the entire room began to cheer.

"Did you think I was going to let you get away from me? It took us all weeks to plan this."

"But . . . but I don't understand . . ."

"I love you," he said. "And thank God for your rules because they made me determined to get you . . ."